String Beans
&
Candy Canes
A Novel

D'Norgia Taylor

PublishAmerica
Baltimore

First printing

At the specific preference of the author, PublishAmerica allowed this work to remain exactly as the author intended, verbatim, without editorial input.

All characters in this book are fictitious, and any resemblance to real persons, living or dead, is coincidental.

ISBN: 1-4241-7709-X
PUBLISHED BY PUBLISHAMERICA, LLLP
www.publishamerica.com
Baltimore

Printed in the United States of America

To write [handwritten]

To Roe,
There are no
accidents and all
things are possible
So often the
greatest
adventures!)

To Leah & Alice
Examine the impossible

Enjoy
D'Souza
Nov 2008

Acknowledgments

There are so many wonderfully fabulous people to thank. First and foremost my comrades Lillian Whitlow, Emma Ford, John Wolfe and Mario DePriest in the Maya Angelou Writers' Guild, I thank you for being there and for the years and hours of talking and reading and critiquing; I thank you for helping me to make this novel a reality. A great big Thank you to Charity Heller-Hogge, my editor, Wow! Lauretta Slaughter, Terri Andrews, Gloria Carter-Wong, and Robert V. Page who encouraged me and helped tremendously, thanks a bunch. Leah Price for critique and Jeffrey Taylor for designing my cover.

Prologue

"If anybody had of asked me and nobody did," Hannah began, "But...I'm gonna tell you anyway." She leaned real close the little ones and continued. "Quiet as it's kept, there are a lot more of us than the official census or anything else, can count. Some of us are real, some maybe not so real. Ya hear me? What I mean is that we don't all leave or arrive the same way and some that we think do, don't. However, we just are!"

The audience of three, four, and five year olds looked at her from what appeared to be just under their eyelashes, with their heads bowed and turned slightly to the right or left, so that they appeared not to be looking at all. Lips tight, eyebrows furrowed and almost touching just above the nose bridge, and rigidly clasped fingers, these little ones huddled together like a brilliantly constructed fortress. Their backs were in a semicircle guarding the window behind them.

She continued, "Now each of you, in your own Time, have to teach and learn and protect, to follow and seek, to correct and love, and mend and watch and grow and heal...and be aware always of danger. If danger approaches you, you must strike if you're the Hammer, endure if you're the Anvil. You will know which is which when the time comes. One of you will always come to each other's aid when the time is right. You always will find each other, no matter who holds you hostage with fear or the appearance of caring. Now, accept your calling according to your heart's song and accept any object from any universe on this table that reminds you of your song."

She walked toward the little ones' place of departure as Shadow trotted behind her like a little puppy and Brid who always was, perched himself on her shoulder. Hannah saw one of the tiny souls finger several of the items before he took his object for his song, and Hannah felt that he may have clipped a piece of something of each object that didn't belong to him. Her insides churned violently for just that instant. She will watch him. He was also trying to memorize others' songs as well. She will have to watch him.

She saw one lingering just a little bit too long as she watched the others gather their new belongings. "Hey, Little Bit, it's time for you to know your whole story. You know you look like a little Floret, yes, a little blossom. "I like the Lily" she said excitedly, just as Baxter picked up that last blossom. "It's gone now," she said as her shoulders drooped down as far as she could sink them.

Hannah handed her a candy cane and told her that she would call her Lily. And just then, Lily heard her song and she was carried away on the whisper she heard and the scent that surrounded her.

Every moment happens at least twice—once at the beginning and at the end; there is a powerlessness of anticipation and change for either time. Lily found her way through.

Chapter 1

Dateline November 8, 2370—This day began crisply, calm and quiet for her. It seemed almost *too* serene when Lily opened her eyes. The morning grabbed her imagination and held it there, in limbo, with anticipation and mystery.

The air felt like it had when her family had vacationed at Wallowa Lake. She had been much younger then. She closed her eyes and could see the clean, dark blue water racing who knows where, a quick white cap at each ripple.

Although the lake, with mountains behind it, had been fascinating, Lily couldn't understand the feelings running through her mind, her racing heart or her prickling skin. She wondered why she was always the one who didn't quite understand most of what was going on without long contemplation or someone pulling her coat to just what was going on. She always seemed to be one step behind and the subject of lots of mistaken perceptions. She read everything she could get her hands on, and especially paid attention to new ideas and information that came her way. But still something surrounded her that was being kept hidden.

The alarm clock hadn't gone off and yet she was wide-awake. She heard birds chirping from the tree just outside, and staring in her window. They were lively with maddening, cheerful chirping and cackles, enjoying their early worm breakfasts. Out the window she looked across the grass and flowers and noticed Kaye's light on. She threw on a top and a pair of slacks over her pajamas so she could go outside for a minute. The air was just right; a nice little bite of lilac hung over the morning.

She ran next door with bare feet and an unwashed face. Kaye, just a few years older, felt like the big sister Lily had always wanted. Lily's folks were glad when Kaye's family moved in, but the little boys who moved away were missed. They were a lot of fun and she teased them by calling them B &C, for their real names, Baxter and Chandler. The move was so sudden she thought, and the memory passed right out of her head. Kaye had already graduated from high school and was studying at the university. Lily also planned to attend there, if she could.

Lily ran on over to her neighbor's house entering through the unlocked door. Hearing laughter, she knew Kaye was already awake. As she walked into Kaye's room, she saw the open door to the attic and saw someone walking up carrying a box. *Hmmm...I wonder what Kaye's doing up there?* She thought, sprinting up the stairs calling Kaye's name. For a quick second Kaye turned around and just as their eyes locked, Kaye simply wasn't there anymore.

Lily felt a fleeting, mischievous smile come from Kaye. *Am I seeing things?* Lily thought as she went back to Kaye's room, where the bed was made and the room straightened just as if she had left for the day. But Lily knew she'd just seen her.

She went up to the stairwell and sat quietly in the attic feeling that the room was alive with *something* but she didn't know what. Had she drifted back off to sleep and just couldn't jump out of a dream? Lily started for the door and felt a chill when she crossed the area where she'd seen Kaye vanish. *That was so weird*, she thought, pinching herself, which didn't help at all.

The prickly skin covering her entire body now made her shiver, and she wasn't sure if she was still dreaming, sleep walking or did Kaye really just disappear before her eyes?

Kaye knew how to do everything; she seemed so wise all the time. She and Lily were inseparable since they first met when Kaye's family moved there, yet were as different as night and day. Everything was great and astonishing about Kaye. Lily accepted her own lack of knowledge, but she burned inside to transform her ordinary days into moments of excitement and wonder and knowledge.

Lily recognized that too little knowledge and too much trust could be dangerous as well as hurtful, and it had been. In everything they'd done together, Kaye seemed to always find the key as if she'd been there, done that before or experienced all that Lily was just finding out. It was wonderful to have such a friend always lead you in the "best" way. But Lily had to figure out how Kaye had so much information.

The girls used to play in Kaye's old attic and Kaye had told Lily that she should read more of the old diaries, letters and pictures that someone left up there and let her know what she thought. She'd never been there without Kaye before…but today the trunk was there, open…and Kaye sure wasn't. She'd just vanished. And, there was a strange little box in the corner, half covered with a scarf.

On the inside lid of the trunk were the instructions, almost demanding her attention, they were quite clear and precise. Lily *did* have an inquisitive nature. The instructions told her to wear the necklace hanging over the second diary…a cute, thin, golden one, which had a charm with her nickname engraved on it, "Gnocchi" it also said to take the instructions with her and the old writing pen but not the diaries or the box that couldn't be opened. A hand written message from Kaye said: H*ave fun, girl, I do. I'll see you in due time—push the button now.*

So she did.

Chapter 2

Dateline November 8, 1997—Jacob graduated from Annapolis and believed it his duty to sign up for a tour in Vietnam. After serving his mandatory military time he couldn't wait to get home and start his life. He left the military with the rank of Major. Even after all he saw, Jacob continued to pursue his education, earning several degrees and accepting a teaching position at the local university. He continued to be troubled by the things he did and saw in the war.

Academic life went a long way toward pushing the hardened bad thoughts into the corners of his mind, but he could not entirely forget the regimen of war.

His wife Grace had contributed more toward helping him recover than anything. But Grace was gone. Grace had been driving home, crossing a bridge after shopping with a friend, when her car was hit or swerved or something like that and it jumped the embankment and landed at the river's edge. By the time help had arrived, her car was fully immersed and her body was nowhere to be found. He felt lost and did not know how he could continue at anything.

Now at the tail end of December, Christmas had come and gone and Jacob sat at Fisher's Point, looking out over the water, thinking about his life. She was gone. The hurt was still there, the anger was still there and the universe had taken his life away.

It was cold on the bench overlooking the water, and Jacob didn't think much about the quiver that went through his body. It was just a chill to him. Like someone was close, but…He looked around and saw no one, but the feeling persisted. He'd had this feeling before, but not since his days in battle. His inner sense told him that an enemy was close by, but this was different because Jacob didn't feel fear. The hair on the back of his neck rose up as if electrified, but fear was not there. Not so much a good or bad feeling, just weird.

He looked around again and shook it off. Down near the cliffs, a couple watched the crests of waves, looking for whales as the sun lay down on the Pacific Ocean. The parking lot was empty except for his car, the couple's car and…a third.

Someone sat inside. He could make out a female looking form, talking on something, maybe a tape recorder. *She may be just looking in a mirror while waiting for a boyfriend or something*, Jacob thought.

He turned his attention back to the couple that was now walking further down the path out of his view and he thought of Grace again. Her cute, diminutive, dark brown figure, sparkling bright dark brown eyes and soft dark hair, cut short after years of wearing it long…God, he missed her. *How am I going to live my life without her?* He thought.

He got up to leave, felt that feeling again and saw the third car leaving the lot. He barely noticed the damaged right rear fender. As the vehicle faded, so did the feeling. But it awoke feelings that had not been stirred for quite a long while. His hunting instinct almost, but it was quickly dismissed.

Jacob drove the long way home, circling the city, driving over as many bridges as his path could take. He enjoyed the short string of curves and rambling homes in the area. He and Grace often talked about buying one on the hill, someday.

Thoughts continued to run through his mind of what could have been.

After Jacob drove across the Gladstone Bridge, he rested his head on the steering wheel until the light changed. Continuing south a few more blocks to his street, there was anticipation in his spirit that he could not account for, so he just made one more loop through the park.

It was dark. The streetlights were on. There seemed to be no one else driving around that night. Everyone on his block parked in his or her driveway or garage, except the guy next door. It seemed that Benny, a recently retired engineer for the power company, had brought everything home with him from the job and stored it in his garage.

Just a few weeks ago, Jacob had told Benny, "Hey, you really ought to clean this out and have a garage sale or something."

Benny smiled skeptically and said, "not yet, there's a gold mind in here. I'm gonna wait til I get my patent on it."

It was a running joke between them, as Jacob parked in the garage and Benny parked outside on the street in front of his driveway. "Benny, the garage is the car's house. Buy a shed or something for all that stuff. Add a room to your house so you could keep all that...whatever it is." Jacob said. Benny just smiled and shook his head.

Chapter 3

Benny was not a large man, more round than tall. The gray at his temples gave him a distinguished look and sometimes he seemed just a bit ruffled. He had moved in the neighborhood with his second wife about four months ago. Cora was buxom bleach blond with not-quite-nappy roots and nice legs. She was probably half Benny's age but she evidently loved him dearly. It was kind of cute, the way they finished each other's sentences.

They had one daughter, a six-year-old named Hannah who was as charming as a kitten and who Cora already had when she met Benny. That was the neighborhood gossip. Who knew for sure and better yet, who was going to ask? Hannah's father, so the story went, had died in a strange accident. He'd been walking along when he choked on something and fell down in the street. He was taken to the hospital and laid in a coma a month before dying, but his body had disappeared before he was officially pronounced dead. When Cora went to claim his body, it was gone. Records indicated he'd been cremated in error. Benny had come along at the right time for Cora, just when he was needed. But then, Cora was there for Benny, too. Hannah, in this Time, was there for them all.

The funeral, or should I say memorial service only attracted the gossips and a couple of co-workers. No one looked for Hannah's father or raised any other questions about what happened to him, after the service, even though there was no evidence of a cremation.

As he pulled into his driveway coming home from the Point, Jacob did not see Benny's car. He hit the button for his garage door and was about to drive in when that feeling hit him again, this time with much more intensity. Jacob thought he heard rushing water. It made his whole body jump. He looked around but saw no one, nothing. Something was wrong, but he couldn't put his finger on it.

He got out of the car, walked to the curb and looked up and down the street, seeing nothing still. Wait. There was one vehicle, half a block down the street.

Although the position of the streetlights prevented Jacob from seeing if anyone was inside, and although it didn't register at the time, he saw the damaged right fender.

Jacob returned to his thoughts, drove inside the garage and lowered the door. As he walked into his living room, Grace's cat, Shadow, met him and rubbed against his ankle, purring hello and demanding to know why he was late. There was food to be served and he had not yet served it. He stroked the cat. It seemed as if Shadow missed Grace, too, and only was willing to be friends now that she was gone. Shadow knew Grace would be coming back, but not when.

Every once in a while Jacob thought about how Shadow just showed up one day and sat at the back door, so Grace fed him. *His appearance actually coincided with Hannah's daily visits,* Jacob thought. This continued for several days until Grace went out and bought him a dish and real cat food and invited him in for as long as he wanted to stay. He pranced in with an attitude that said, "What took you so long?"

Shadow had been a stray, one of Grace's many successful projects. Grace had taken him in against Jacob's better judgment. Jacob and Shadow had never made their friendship work before, but things were different now.

16

Jacob walked out the front door to get the mail. At first he didn't notice the small package on the porch. He opened the mailbox and that feeling hit him again. He looked directly at the car. There was something about that car up the block. Something he could not put his finger on, something that he was supposed to recognize. What was it? He walked back to the house and watched the car drive away slowly.

As he turned to close the door, it hit him. He turned quickly and looked, "the fender" damage indicated that was the same car he had seen at Fisher's Point. Something was wrong. The car...what was it? A Chrysler, but not one he readily recognized. There was something strange about the car that he couldn't quite get his mind to recognize, and it was definitely the same one he had seen earlier that evening. It would come to him, he thought, pushing the feeling away. *Maybe it's just a crazy student prank.*

He stepped onto the porch and noticed Shadow rubbing against the package, purring curiously and fighting with its string. It was wrapped in plain brown paper and was addressed to "Professor Jacob Nobel," but had no return address or post mark. He stared in the direction of the car as the streetlights just came fully alive. *Did someone in that car leave me this package*? He thought.

"Hi Mr. Jacob," said Hannah from the edge of her driveway. He smiled and just waved back. It's strange that he didn't notice her walking away from the direction of that mysterious car.

Jacob took the mail, papers to be recycled and package into his den. He set them on the desk near his computer and began opening the mail. Bills...more bills...some credit card offers...a letter from the church memorial committee. It was a personalized mailer, advertising really a form letter, thanking him for allowing them to serve in his time of grief. *I am still grieving* he thought. *Where are you now?"* He tossed the brochure into the wastebasket by his desk, knowing he would retrieve it in an hour. It was just his statement for the moment.

A heavy sigh escaped him as he thought about how he could get rid of this funky feeling. If he didn't, he was going to drive himself into an early demise, too. That would be ok with him. He tossed the rest of the mail onto the desk, covering the package, and picked up the students' papers that needed to be graded right away.

His class: He had almost forgotten about during the last few weeks. These were the term papers for the first class of "Anthropological and Modern Historical Research."

It was essentially an introduction to some of his hobbies and pet peeves about history, between 1400 and 1966. He had tried to convince the dean for several semesters to allow him to teach it, but had been turned down for years. Finally, he'd been allowed to teach it and found the students were interested in just digging up old dirt, quite invigorating.

He had a huge stack of papers to grade that he had not considered when assigning the project. The students were to pick a historical event from any time period and conduct analytical research justifying a hypothesis. It was quite difficult to remove the fantasy and rumor and get down to the hard facts that analytical research demanded. The events chosen had to have some controversy in which the real truth had always been questioned and challenged. He hoped to get a feel for the students' takes on how the events or the propaganda of the events shaped respective societal norms. How much of the past did these students hold true as reported, and which did they dispute?

The first paper was from a young Latino named Tony Grijaleva. Tony was extremely bright and intuitive, majoring in Business Administration. His family believed that Tony would take over his father's business after he finished school. They owned several small grocery markets in the area;

however. Tony had confided that he had bigger plans that didn't include the family business.

Jacob looked at the paper: "Amelia is Alive and Traveled Though Time to give us a Message." The title surprised him. He thought for a moment and began reading. It was Tony's belief that Amelia Earheart had not died in a plane crash. Her body had never been recovered because she came from a different time and could recreate herself as often as needed and vacate any dangerous situations with very little effort. She and an aid, according to Tony, had escaped, unknown to everyday people, but the others who knew, believed that she had gone back to her own time. *This is ridiculous*, thought Jacob.

Tony identified many others who disappeared without a trace or who met untimely deaths that were not associated with foul play, and whose bodies disappeared or were moved mysteriously.

The paper went on to describe a very possible escape route of Hitler; how he'd changed into civilian clothes and used forged papers to slip behind American lines with refugee Jews being released from a box car, as American soldiers approached from the west. Once outside German lines, it was easy to escape to Switzerland, where he hid for years. Finally in the late '50's, he went to Afghanistan where many of the Third Reich soldiers retired or disappeared.

Many showed up in the United States with new identities and new faces. The bodies they found were corpses taken from another time.

Jacob thought about the content of Tony's paper, noting that it did actually cover all the points that he identified for grading. He scanned over highlights of the paper, made a couple of red marks and decided that Tony earned a "C" for his effort, however, he noted that Tony would have to improve the final draft to include more convincing literary comments, interviews and hard science documentation.

There was not enough scientific evidence presented. It was well written grammatically, but not a good paper in terms of argument because there was not enough research cited to prove his conclusion. There was no such thing as time travel and no real viable proof was offered. *Just because you say it, doesn't make it so.* Jacob thought.

He was about to pick up another paper when Shadow jumped on his desk and began purring and prancing around, raising his back and tail high in the air to get Jacob's attention. The cat knocked the letters off the brown package and Jacob once again let curiosity get the better of him. He picked up the package.

Hannah's voice could be heard from her backyard, humming her song just outside Jacob's window. It was a rather sweet tune. He stopped and listened for a moment. "It's way too late for that child to be outside," he said to Shadow.

He read his name again on the package and turned it over several times looking for a return address or any clue about its origin. None. He sniffed it, weighed it in his hands, one hand then the other, trying to guess what it contained. He looked at Shadow. "What do you think, fella, should I open it?" Shadow purred approvingly, so Jacob tore the wrapping away from the object. It was an odd kind of paper, even…tissue paper thin, but you couldn't see through it and it unraveled when balled up.

He tossed it straight ahead as it sailed like an airplane that opened mid flight into the wastebasket near his desk. *Two points*, he thought, and quickly retrieved the wrapping. He removed the lid of the black box. Inside was what looked like a pocket calculator or transistor radio or maybe a tape recorder. The item inside the box had three large gold letters on the top lid: TTC. He did not recognize that as a company and opened the TTC. It certainly looked like a transistor radio; he had seen one pretty much like this at one of those stores. *Who makes this brand? Sharp, Casio?*

The keyboard looked normal but odd on a radio, having a few extra buttons he didn't immediately recognize. Just below the screen, he saw something printed in small gold letters: "Time Travel Coordinator." He looked inside the box at least there was a "how to" book. The small paperback had 'TTC' printed on the cover and what appeared to be several different models that looked real. He saw **"XII VIII XXIIIC (expiration)"** below the keyboard in tiny print. *A date, maybe?* He thought. *Hmmm, December 8, 2370? No that can't be right.*

Jacob looked in the box again and found a letter. The odd-looking envelope was addressed to him. It was scented but not sealed. Shadow lay on the desk giving him that furry-eyed stare that said nothing but aloofness.

He opened the letter and began to read: "Dear Professor Nobel, you may not remember that you've met me, and that's ok..." his eyes blurred and he couldn't read any further. He knew the handwriting.

Chapter 4

Jacob set the letter down on his desk and stared at it for a long time. Was this some kind of joke? It had to be, there was no such thing as time travel, let alone a machine the size of a wallet or transistor radio that could accomplish it.

The letter mentioned a book, and he now focused on what was still in the box. The title was clear enough, but his eyes focused further on the author's name. He blinked but the name didn't change: it was even sharper now and burning into his eyes "Jacob Nobel." *Someone had gone to great expense to set up such an elaborate joke.* Jacob thought. *Tony must have done this to prove a point!* "But what?" Just leaped out of his mouth.

The book was titled *Real History, A Second Time* which was strange; Jacob had thought of that as a title for a book some years ago. Had he given that information to someone who was now playing a joke on him?

The book was well bound in dark maroon leather with bright gold lettering. It appeared to be very old, but when he flipped to the second page he saw at the bottom of the page, Putnam Books, a division of Random House, New York, 2004.

He almost dropped the book. He turned it over and inspected it again. It was much, older than he originally thought. *But how can the date be 2004? It is still 1996; well it will soon be '97, but still, this book has not been printed yet, according to the information inside the cover.*

He picked up the letter again and read the signature at the bottom; *Lily.* He read the letter again this time a little slower making sure he was understanding everything that he read. According to the letter Lily, was in the year 2296, 300 years from Jacob's time, but according to the jacket, he had published this book many years from right now. The book had become a best seller and had changed a lot of people's ideas about truth, history and government.

Jacob set the book and letter back on his desk. He got up and walked to the large picture window overlooking the shallow lake behind his home. He stared into gray mist now closing in on the water. The foghorn from the lighthouse a mile up the shoreline could be heard bellowing its deep-pitched warning.

The letter had been particularly disturbing to him because beneath the writer's signature was a little squiggly sign, looped at both ends with fancy curls and 3 vertical lines down through the middle. It was an unusual way of punctuating one's signature. Grace had always done her signature that way. The sign was almost identical.

He stared into the night fog then abruptly turned, walked to his desk and opened the top drawer. He rifled through papers and bill receipts for a few moments until he found it all the way back in the corner of the drawer. He gently retrieved it: a letter Grace had written when she went to San Francisco last year. She had stayed almost two weeks and wrote him a very long letter, telling him that she loved him and of all the things she'd seen and the tours she'd taken and the things she planned to buy and bring home and, at the end how she missed him. She signed her name and there it was, the squiggly sign, looped at both ends with fancy curls and three vertical lines. He held both the papers up together to the light and compared them. They were almost identical. He let both letters drop to the desk as goose bumps raced up his spine. He just held his breath a moment and threw glances all about the room. His swallow dried in his throat as he ran through the house, looking in every room and turning on all the lights.

Who was this Lily person, and what was she trying to do to him? Grace was dead. Her body had been lost in the river after the auto accident, and now some stranger comes along saying come to the future and signed her name like Grace. How was that possible, how is any of this possible? Did he dare believe any of this? *I'm crackin' up!* Jacob thought. *I must be.*

He paced back and forth across the office floor. Shadow stared at him from atop the desk as he walked from one side of the room to the other. Jacob's mind jumped from the book, to the letter, to the TTC. Was any of this true and if so, how? There was no such thing as time travel and if there were, surely it wouldn't be done with a radio! He turned slowly and stared at the papers he'd just graded and remembered Tony's. *It's just a joke,* he thought. But his heart didn't believe his thoughts.

Lily's letter said she was in the year 2396. Well, it could be. The Japanese have made great advances in technology. So maybe so. He thought..."Maybe so," he said out loud and jumped at hearing his own voice.

Jacob's head whirled with thought, *well ok, ya gullible jackass, if you are so smart, figure out how this thing works and go for a spin.* He picked up the user guide and opened it to the table of contents. He began reading down the long list, introduction, about this guide, additional information, special notes to, *aha,* Chapter *one, a) set up. page 1.1. I'm gonna try this.*

Jacob turned to the listed page and began reading. *Well it all seems rather simple...Configure my body dimensions by placing my hand over the light and allow the contraption to put them in memory.* He checked his pulse rate and entered the numbers in the proper sequence. He then entered his body weight, blood type, age, name and height and pressed the "store" button. Then he watched as little diode lights below the screen signaled that something was going on. The screen lit up and read; Time travel functions for Jacob Nobel set, 1996/0012/27/1905 hrs. Jacob thought. *This seems easy enough. It could be interesting if it works, or a neat new board game like Clue or find the Idiot.*

Jacob wondered for a moment. *Where would I go in time, what is it I want to see?* He remembered the car he had seen driving away. *How long ago was that…twenty minutes, a half hour…no, at least an hour. If this thing works*, he thought, *I'll go back and take a better look at that car and see who was driving it.*

He found the information regarding location and entered it, a location a half-block from his house. With coordinates from a global satellite locator, a change in location of 50 yards registered. He typed in all of the pertinent information and stood there for a few moments. *Well,* he thought, *here goes nothing.*

Jacob felt movement immediately.

The room around him seemed to drift away from him in all directions and he felt a slight queasiness in his stomach as if he were aboard ship. The room suddenly disappeared and there was darkness. A sudden fear of the unknown hit him and he questioned his own sanity as to what he had done. He noticed a light a long way off and it suddenly became brighter. He wanted to run but his legs would not move. When the light became clear, he recognized the streetlight, like on his block.

He looked down the street and was reassured to see his house. He was about to start walking in that direction when he remembered the reason he had made this test was to see the car. He quickly turned and saw it pulling away from the curb. The driver was a woman.

The car pulled into a driveway near where he stood, backed out, and drove away. As it passed him, the driver looked at him in surprise. He did not recognize her but obviously she recognized him. *Who is she? Does she have anything to do with all of this?* He thought about the look on her face. Maybe she was just startled because she did not expect anyone to be in the driveway as she turned around, or maybe...*no, it's not a figment of my imagination* he thought. *This is real!*

As the car moved away, Jacob could see the license plate and the tag and immediately knew something else was wrong. He knew he had not recognized the car when he first saw it but believed it to look like a Chrysler, one of the smaller, luxury models. But he knew, too, having explored an interest in new cars that he had never seen this model before. The tags read, "Dec 1999." The car slowed for a second as the driver tried to appear not to look directly at him and he glared at her, partly in amazement.

The car turned the corner and was out of sight. Jacob was returned to reality by the sound of the foghorn in the harbor. He looked around then and started walking back toward his house. *Wait a minute,* he thought. *If I walk home I will still be 60 minutes in the past, and may run into myself in the house. What had the warning read about PARADOX?* He looked down at the TTC in his hand, remembered the procedure in the instructions and pushed the return and enter button. Suddenly he was whisked away; he noticed someone else was there, just in the corner of his left eye.

When his swimming head had settled down he was sitting at his desk again in his office. The TTC diodes flashed and finally settled on a yellow light for "standby." He looked around the room. Everything seemed the same; nothing had moved. Shadow still sat on his desk looking at him as if he had never left. *Well,* he wondered, *did I leave, or is this all some gigantic hoax? But I saw the car and I saw the woman driving.*

I will not *soon forget her,* he thought. *She was strange yet familiar.* The TTC had returned him to the exact moment, the next tick in time after he left. It was like he had never left. He knew in his heart, although he did not want to believe it, it *actually worked.* He had traveled back in time, albeit only for a few minutes. If only he could talk with PawPaw about this. Where the hell was he?

This time he would remember his travel.

Chapter 5

November 8, 1970—Now, only two people knew about this and only one of them remembered...that in a far away time and place, Jacob was going through Grandpa's things again, he had so much interesting stuff. Wow! He knew so much, too. But from time to time, he just disappeared for a while. It was said that sometimes he'd even show up looking younger and more debonair than when they last saw him! He said he had found the fountain of youth. *Yeah right*, thought Jacob. The dream last night he had of Grandpa was so vivid, "PawPaw," he called him.

Pawpaw talked of people he knew, but he could not have possibly been alive to remember some of them. Jacob always questioned his trips and was told; "One day you'll have a fire in your heart to know beyond today." Jacob thought that very weird, but that was PawPaw——he was a bit strange.

Jacob was angry and apprehensive today, anyway. On TV lately, many of the images were still of the riots over the killing of Martin Luther King, Jr., and Bobby Kennedy, student demonstrations against the war, students killed at Kent State, dying soldiers in Vietnam and political corruption. There was so much dying in Vietnam, the election of Nixon and other corruption. It was crazy. He wondered if he'd have to go to war and if his application to Annapolis would be accepted.

Stretching as far as his arms could reach and then pulling up from the headboard, Jacob tried to rid his sleepy eyes of the cobwebs he felt before he could open them. He jumped down to the floor to do his sit-ups and push-ups, then more stretching. "Whew!" His own voice was the first sound he heard that morning.

Food, food, food, he thought. He looked for the quickest stuff he could push in his face to end the growls active in his entire torso and cereal would work, he'd eat it dry if there was no milk. "Bingo" came another burst from his throat, which surprised him again. Milk, cereal, bananas and nuts...*everything's here,* he thought as he surveyed the fridge. The day was starting off great! He took his breakfast with him to the den so he could catch sports news before he left.

His face didn't come up from the bowl until it was just about dishwater clean. He picked up the cereal box for another bowl and a stab at the puzzle on the back of the box and to see what the stuff he just ate was made of, but stopped when he noticed the diaries there on the table. They hadn't been there when he fixed his first bowl. He turned to see where that sound of water came from, the sink was dry, and he knew he'd turned the shower off, tight.

He stared at the diaries for a moment and reached his hand over to touch one as if he were just about to pet a snake. Several tiny jerks in his hand and wrist made it a very slow and reluctant process. He looked around—the air felt strange— then looked back at the books. They were still thick with dust, and there were no prints from being handled. He saw the note atop the diaries, and recognized PawPaw's handwriting. "Dear Jacob, evidently the fire has started, otherwise you would not be in this space at this moment. Remember that you can't hold time, and that the consequences of changing the events of time will ignite a fire to disaster and break your heart." He told Jacob to read the diaries then read page 2 of the note. The instructions on the next page of the note were clear and precise. Jacob did have an inquisitive nature. He was instructed to wear the bracelet with his name on it, enclosed in the package under the diaries, but to leave the box there. The handwritten message from PawPaw also said, "Have fun, Boy, I do. I'll see you in due time—push the button now."

So he did.

Jacob and Lily had now both discovered the secrets of Kaye and PawPaw, and realized that same inner power. The same power used by a new seedling to break through the soil. The soil that restrains it from basking in sunlight was the same power they must draw upon to break into and out of the time channel.

Only one of them remember this event, and even though they did not quite fully understand what they'd stumbled into at the time, a plan had already been set into motion and they were on their way through time. However, no one knew this fire would start between them. PawPaw blamed himself.

Lily wanted to go back in time to see what she could see and just what it all felt like. She wanted to learn about the past to discover the reason things were the way they were now, and maybe to bring back new lessons to teach others. Her search had begun. Lily realized that this was what Kaye was trying to get her to see all this time. She had always known that there was something she was supposed to know and be a part of…but this was so far from any of her imagining; her thoughts still could not quite grasp it all. It was like finding a piece of a puzzle that you had no idea even existed.

At the time, Jacob thought he could go forward and see what life would be like in the future and how the events of today that he watched on television would unravel. Would America win the war? Would the murderer of the Rev. Dr. Martin Luther King be found and convicted? Was the Kennedy assassination part of a conspiracy? How would Vietnam affect their lives? Would students be afraid to protest because of fear of the National Guard? What was the real power of social engineering and how was it greater than the simple power of persuasion? His thoughts often took him back to an old children's story called "The Emperor's New Clothes." Why was a child the only one to point out that the Emperor wasn't wearing any clothes? Could honesty and truth only come from an innocent?

All of this was going on and a child watched in plain view but no one even noticed. She was right there.

Social engineering began in the beginning of time; it was the process of the power to plan, develop and set up systems that allowed some to have and some to have-not. Social Engineering made it possible to identify the workers and the privileged, the rulers and those to be ruled. It also directed social change to which ever group they wanted to exploit for a time and turn everyone's attention to them and not what was really at hand. They knew when to create alliances and when to wage war, based on which plots of land could be overtaken for its resources. Natural resources went in and out of being chic. It was gold, and then land, it was territory, and then water, iron and the sun and then it was oil and natural gas, only to go back to land, water and clean air, the way it was in the beginning.

By 2255, the pollution was too severe and oxygen, scarce. So there was no going back, only now they could actually capture another planet that was discovered in 2007. But, they had to harness time. And, they had to decide who was expendable. Those who went first may not ever come back.

Both, Jacob and Lily, now each in different times, understood the rituals and went into their deep fog, making themselves aware of the molecular breakdown of their physical beings. They both ascended, each unaware of the other in the same dimension chamber. Speeding over and through 1970, Jacob and Lily in 2370, glided, joined and collided with such a force and intensity that the instant their souls met, they shared a breath of a second that made them one soul, one person, neither had known before or would ever again. A tiny piece of each was left with the other. They would always hold past and future memories of the other, never knowing from where the information came.

Upon reaching ground at home in her own realm, Lily found that her necklace was missing, but discovered a bracelet on her ankle when she made her re-entry; it read "Jacob," and made a mark just above her anklebone. Jacob's bracelet was gone but around his neck, almost choking him, a tiny chain with a charm and name on it, "Gnocchi," had left a mark just below his ear.

Lily walked and tumbled and floated through all the times she wanted. There were no ordinary days for her, and she discovered many secrets of the universe, marveled and understood.

Jacob learned that Martin Luther King's murderer was convicted and that although he had to go to war, he came home with an honorable discharge. He was accepted to study at some military school, something that he so desperately wanted. He decided to go back and live his own life, this present life, and it was good.

Lily wanted to make the trip again to see if she could find the owner of the bracelet. She'd talk with Kaye about it.

Jacob wondered about the necklace and the sudden appearance of a deep scar under his ear; he knew it couldn't be a birthmark, although it appeared to have been there forever. He would not soon conscientiously remember any of his travels in time or his collision with Lily.

The little girl also witnessed it all. She had the kind of face you see in a crowd, a familiar face, and a smile that you can't quite place.

Chapter 6

The first time Lily had actually traveled it made her sick. She had not known what to expect, however, and the queasiness that had occupied her stomach soon dissipated. Travel became easier each time she tried it. This time was no different. She sat, just letting it all settle, her mind settled back into 1996. It still amazed her, the fact that she could do it at all. When Professor Stevens explained the whole theory to her. Amazingly, she'd understood.

He had been helpful in her quest, warning her of what could happen. She knew not to make direct contact, thereby causing the possibility of some sort of paradox occurring in her own time. She was strictly an observer...with some minor modifications. Her own personal mission was to get Jacob to her time.

She wanted to find out from him just what he knew. She wanted to work with him, and to tell him how much she had learned from his books on history and no, she could not tell him her identity, not yet. She didn't really know what she felt herself, but knew something was missing. She only knew that she wanted to bring him back to her time because she could not stay in his and cause the type of paradox that Professor Stevens had described.

What a dilemma. But she was solving it. She had conceived a plan to get him the technology, the small pieces of equipment, so that he, too, could travel in time. With a few hints and some direction on her part, he would soon be in her time, working with her on the many things that they had in common. She could not tell him about her other identity, not yet, anyway, only because she didn't quite know all of it herself. She knew that they collided on their first trip. But still she wondered who kept removing his memory of his time in other dimensions and his knowledge of how to get there. That thought gave her an instant chill, too fleeting to dwell upon.

She looked at the equipment her professor had given her. It seemed so innocent. One might mistake it for a simple transmitter or keyboard, though it was much smaller. It opened like a keyboard and had a screen much like an old television viewer. She remembered the first one she had seen at the institute. It was large and cumbersome and reminded her of HG Well's time machine from three or four centuries ago. The traveler had to sit encircled by tubes and lights and gadgets. Then a few years later, they came up with the helmet. Then the laptop to pocket pouch. All she had to do was punch in the coordinates, time and the dimensions. Then she input the mass of the object that she was taking with her (the car in this case) and then press Enter. Yes, it had all been so easy this time.

The car was a cinch to nab. She'd found it abandoned and transported it forward to a time where she restored it quickly, then brought it back with her to 1996. *Piece of cake*, she thought and laughed out loud.

She now sat at this place...what was the name, Fishers' Point, just watching him. This was the seventh or eighth time she had gone back and watched, but had never come this close. He acted like he knew she was there, glancing around. She picked up the TTC and spoke the directions into memory, just in case she had to leave quickly.

Maybe it was time to leave, she thought, and then decided to deliver the package to his house rather than just leaving it in his car. Driving there might be difficult, but she could not just transport from the parking lot with other people, including him, milling around. She pulled out of the parking lot and then initiated the transporter to take her forward in time. She set the destination dial for a block away from Jacob's house, and the time for five minutes ahead...but before she knew it, he'd arrived.

It was getting dark now that the sun had set. The streetlights were all lighting up. Looking around, Lily saw no one...but heard dogs barking a block away.

The moon was faint over the city's harbor and that left lights shimmering between the masts of sailboats in the marina. The masts danced back and forth like tin soldiers, each marching to a tune of their own. Waves lapped at the funnels of the small crafts making a silent dance heard only by the incoming fog and seagulls marching on the beach.

A small tanker was moving from the harbor, it's horn sounding boldly at the gathering fog. She shivered, hugged herself and silently cursed for not wearing warmer clothing. *Next time,* she thought.

It was cool but not cold for December, and little goose bumps were forming on the back of her neck as she anticipated her next move. Everything up to this point had just been observation, as Professor Stevens said, but now she was actually going to give him the Time Travel Coordinator. Jacob would understand the directions and know how to use the TTC. It was really quite simple. She'd grown in her ability to move back and forth through time without disturbing anyone or anything. Well, not quite. The car, she thought, was brilliant. Okay, maybe just smart. Once he had the TTC, he would rush forward in time to see his benefactress. She would be waiting.

Jacob did not remember his first travel experience. In fact, he would remember none of them. PawPaw made sure of that. PawPaw knew immediately by the gleam in Jacob's eye that he would try to make things different, so PawPaw decided to re-program the travel to have Jacob come back at the moment just before he got his cereal and milk and he read the note from him, so he would never remember. Each time PawPaw found out that Jacob had taken an adventure with Lily, PawPaw re-programmed Jacob's memory.

Then suddenly Jacob was just there, in front of Lily, standing in a driveway watching her intently as she turned to drive away. This piece was definitely not in the plan; he must have gone into the house, used the TTC and come back in time to see who she was. This was not expected. She watched in the rear view mirror while driving away. He just stood there, staring in her direction.

Had this changed anything? She thought for a moment. No, it just means that he is as smart as I always thought and he now was even more curious about who I am. Enough so, that he immediately used the TTC to find out about the car and me...No need to panic, she thought. He would be coming to find her soon. She was still curious about why he stared at the car so intently.

Getting rid of the car was too easy. Lily just returned it just where she found it, and no one would ever missed it. It was just an old, abandoned car left in a place that people discarded a lot of their unwanted appliances and junk hoping someone else would dispose of it.

Lily did not think about the fact that she had obtained the car from the year 1999. There were many places like that when she went back in time. Places where people had used up all the resources they could get out of an area, and once used up, they'd find a new place to settle. The abandoned area would be used to house whatever was to be thrown away: all sorts of garbage, bankrupt business leftovers, furniture and people. Whatever society wanted to throw out, could be found on the side of the road. Lily found the throw-a-ways interesting because she wanted to find out about the life of their existence. The places, the people and the things they threw away.

Yes, it was all becoming easier for Lily, a habit she was going to have to break. She was becoming hooked but didn't realize it. A drug in the form of time was seducing her little by little. It was ironic, because she had been locked into her own time for so long, and the other time took her memory and ability to travel. What was it that enticed her back there now? There was something here she needed to know and her realm wasn't ready to let her know what she was looking for, but it was close.

Her arrival home was uneventful, with one exception. She felt invigorated because they had seen each other in his time, eyeball to eyeball.

Her letter started: *"Dearest Jacob, we have known each other throughout your future and in both our pasts. You have known me well since childhood, and there are answers to your many questions about what really happened in certain historical events. I know the answer to some of your questions."*

He'd only gone to look at the car but did not follow her home, even though she left specific instructions and directions for him to find her in her time. *What was wrong?* She wondered.

Jacob needed to speak with PawPaw. The last time he'd seen him he was in a strange state of mind. PawPaw had mentioned a friend of his, a colleague named Katherine, and she was missing.

That was a long while ago. Jacob wondered if he could remember the date and location, then perhaps find him there. PawPaw's old diaries would tell him, but the diaries were no longer in the place Pawpaw always left them. For now, Jacob needed to find out more about Lily.

Chapter 7

After the Package

Jacob stared at the letter for what seemed like forever—he wanted it to all be a bad dream, a horrible dream, a dream with an end. "Oh, God, please let me wake from this," he spoke out loud. His gaze fell to the floor and he stood there with nothing to hold on to. No railing, no chair arm, no desk—in the middle of the floor he stood—no one. He fought back tears because his heart hurt so. He just stayed quietly wrapped in every one of his dreams of Grace. His shoulders drooped, and with head down he moved to the sofa; he sat in his corner and breathed in a long, deep breath, then reluctantly pushed it out and tried not to think how he wanted to remain totally empty. Jacob continued roaming his mind for his warmest thoughts, a longing that he carried with him in everything he did. He searched his memory and found the day he first met her.

It was on the north end of the campus, on a beautiful sunny day. They were walking on a path that led to the Administration building and the parking lot. Neither of them was paying attention to the present; they were just trying to get to where they wanted to be. They collided with a *bam!*

She dropped her books and papers and he dropped his, and all their stuff was entangled. Well, she was already late for class and he was finished for the day, so he invited her for a cup of coffee to untangle and reorganize their papers. She offered a coquettish smile and almost said out loud, " I can see your spirit and somehow I know who you are."

Jacob was at a loss for words at that point so he stumbled upon an apology, begging her pardon for the clumsy accident he caused. Again, with the coy little half smile she said, "Ya know, there are no accidents." She didn't bother to explain— for the moment.

That apology over coffee lasted hours and afterward he just could not get her out of his thoughts. She'd gone deeper than under his skin, and he knew he was powerless but had to mask how he felt, at least to himself. He loved her since before he knew her name, or where she lived, or her major, or her sign, or anything that was her favorite. *Is this what happens*, he thought. She was as lovely as a gentle feather, a soft touch that held him like a welcomed vise. Whenever he saw her, he imagined a magic carpet ride though the clouds and he owned the world, with her forever by his side, his 'familiar.' When she was not with him he imagined her there. And she was.

The whirlwind courtship lasted only a few days, when she agreed to marry him; he realized that she had no family and not much of an identifiable past. She told him how a social worker told her she was found abandoned under a bridge and no one ever claimed her for a long while. Then she was just passed around to several families. There was no clue as to whom she belonged. He vowed to be all she'd ever need, and he kept his promise.

Jacob's eyes fell on the opposite end of the sofa. Her place. She liked to put her feet on his. She would stretch out delicately on the sofa and still make room for him. She liked her projects; she painted and made rugs out of old cloth and yarn, crocheted hats out of string and cut up squares of material to make quilts. Then there was her music. She loved the cello; it made a haunting, beckoning sound and her eyes were a magnet to his when she played, but she focused elsewhere. Always, elsewhere.

His five foot eleven inch frame cradled her when he noticed those elsewhere glances. "What's the matter?" he'd ask. Her answer was always, "I don't know."

Many of their special evenings began in late afternoons, when he would read to her. She liked plays. Lorraine Hansberry was her favorite playwright. She especially liked "Young, Gifted and Black." She liked the poetry of Counte Cullen, Paul Lawrence Dunbar; and all the writings of Zora Neal Hurston, J. California Cooper and Toni Morrison. She listened as intently to his favorites and even memorized some as she did her own, just because she loved him. She wanted to know about everything that made him happy, or brought some sort of joy to his spirit, not realizing that she need do nothing but just 'exist' and the knowledge of her just being, brought him to perfect bliss, ecstasy and a total rapture of his very soul. When she sat near him, he tickled her toes as he read to her. She giggled and the sound illuminated their existence.

"She can't be gone," Jacob cried out loud as his thoughts came back to now.

Chapter 8

Who is Lily, Really?

They talked incessantly, Professor Stevens and Lily, about this and that—tidbits of her life and his. He was constantly asked question after question about her Aunt Kaye, who wasn't Lily's blood relative at all, just a close family friend. He believed Kaye might be the friend of his who was now missing. She was a scientist, too, and they had been close, very close friends. Professor Stevens thought it was strange the way Lily said Kaye was just one day a part of her life, although she had been a silent benefactor since Lily moved, when the last family she lived with was just gone one day. .

He also knew about Lily being abandoned and there seemed to be something familiar about her, as if he knew who her real people were.

Lily was curious to know anything regarding her background. Aunt Kaye's books were a curiosity to the professor even more so now than before, but Lily had not gone through Kaye's things yet…it was still too painful. She didn't know why she couldn't look, but things were not all in place for her yet.

Aunt Kaye had left everything she owned to Lily, with a special emphasis on her diaries and books. Toward the end, no one could really understand Aunt Kaye's jabber—

sometimes the events she described had happened centuries ago, but she spoke of them as if she had just been there and remembered it rather than studied it. Most people thought Kaye had to be senile, that was all there was to it. The professor knew there was more, much more.

Lily was her heart; her best friend in the world and Kaye protected and doted on her as if she were her very own child. While searching the entire globe, on one of her trips, Kaye had found Lily in a new realm. Kaye's family agreed to help raise her so Kaye could continue some special research. Kaye even named her after her dearest and closest friend, Lily Grace. Kaye supposedly vanished just after Lily was discovered abandoned. There were always lots of presents and gadgets in neatly wrapped packages tied with ribbon for Lily. Lily believed she had her own special Santa Claus. She liked the ribbons that were wrapped around the gifts—especially purple and green ones.

One of their mind-boggling conversations came to Lily while she stood in front of the bathroom mirror washing her face. It seemed as though Kaye just appeared out of nowhere—which really wasn't all that unusual—and looking Much older than she had the last time they talked. Kaye began answering Lily's questions and telling her other things she needed to learn.

"Where did all these pimples come from?" she said to Kaye while she scrubbed her face.

"What's the matter?" she asked Lily.

"I don't know why this keeps happening to me. I haven't been eating greasy food or sweets or anything like that and now my face is breaking out again."

"So, where have you been?" Kaye asked.

" Oh, just here and there."

"Where?"

"I went to Atlanta. I wanted to see the peach blossoms."

"Was it muggy? I mean, was the air full of water and dirt?"

"Sort of."

"You go to a café or someone's place to eat?" Kaye inquired.

"Yeah, I ate hush puppies and sausage, but it wasn't greasy."

"Lord, chil' that stuff is cooked in grease and in fact it's made out of greasy animal parts even before it's cooked!"

" It had a really good taste to it." Lily smiled. "Hmmm, hmmm. Now my face is breaking out with this fine rash and stuff and it makes my face so blotchy looking, ya know?"

"You either ate something, or you've been in an adverse atmosphere, or you have had some stress that you are keeping inside."

"Oh, yeah? Well, that little bit of food I ate couldn't have caused this. Also, I can't understand why my neck is still so dirty when I've already cleaned it."

"Your neck? All over?"

"No, just the front here." Answered Lily.

"Keep wiping it with alcohol."

"Why alcohol?" Lily wanted to know.

"You gotta keep that dirt out of that area and that part of your neck needs a little extra help."

"What 'cha mean, I mean, why is that?"

Kaye took a deep breath and said, "That dirt that comes out the front of your neck is from those words that get stuck in your throat that don't need to be said, so you gotta get rid of them however you can. Clean them away with alcohol or witch hazel, otherwise they stay with you and hurt someone that shouldn't hear them."

"Why didn't I know about that before now?"

"Cause your ears would not have heard, and your mind would not have understood it the right way."

Lily turned from the mirror where she saw Kaye's image, but she was alone, even the hallway was empty and left no trace of Kaye's presence.

Professor Stevens encouraged Lily to read the books and study the diaries Kaye had left her. He really wanted to know about the contents but did not want to alert Lily to his intense curiosity. He had known a woman named Kaye, long ago as his contemporary and colleague. That had been before Lily and Kaye searched for secrets and Lily's experiment, which not only took her and Kaye back in time but also took Lily, back in actual years—to infancy. Although many believed baby Lily to be the child of Kaye and the professor, she was really Kaye's oldest and dearest friend.

The professor wanted to unlock the formula for Lily's experiment from her mind. If he pushed too hard and revealed to her the other lives she'd led, he might never find out what happened when all hell had broke loose and Stevens' realm had been almost totally destroyed along with most of the people he loved.

Only Lily knew and could decipher the scripts in the diaries, which were, in fact, Lily's own notes. The professor knew there was another player in all this chaos, but could not find the person. He thought that Jacob, whose bracelet Lily had kept in a locked music box, just might be that person.

Lily slowly closed her coordinator without finding Jacob anywhere in his own time system, or his natural birth realm. She decided to go to his house and wait for him while searching for evidence of where he could be. She just couldn't believe that he had anything to do with anyone's disappearance, not the way Professor Stevens recorded it in his audio diary, she just happened to overhear.

***

The outer corners of Lily's large brown mysterious eyes drooped in sadness Shadow tiptoed playfully across her feet. Lily's sudden appearances no longer startled him into elevating his tail and hissing. He accepted her...no, welcomed her presence. He rubbed his little black furry body around her ankles. Shadow was a great distraction from her worry. There were no pet animals in her time now because each and every living thing was contained and resources like air and water were scarce. Most people kept only those things that produced resources, and became attached to them. They played with butterflies and bees, because they assist pollination, and their plants were perfect pets.

There were a few zoos where animals were kept, and the extinct ones were stuffed or plasticized and could be seen in museums. As the larger animals died off, taxidermy became a profitable business. Many times if a household used up an exceptional amount of food, neighbors suspected someone was caring for an animal. Sometimes those who felt their own resources were dwindling because of this "inconsiderate household" would notify the authorities of irregularities of certain houses.

The underground would go into full force then and any person in the house who got wind of what was happening, called a friend who'd call a friend and the animal would just disappear for a time. No questions. Then the original person who notified the owner would receive some treasured gift from the animal owner and who knows where it went from there. No one ever asked.

Lily continued to wait for Jacob because she knew he wanted to undo the death of his military buddy even though the chaos created by this event might haunt him forever. She couldn't let him know she was actually one of the 'others,' He thought she was just a companion from another time. So now she could go to the battlefield or home to year 2396 and let it all play out in horror, or do exactly as he did and change time's course for thousands of the next un-born.

She considered leaving a note for him to meet her atop the pyramids and go wait for him. She knew the note would again feel like an introduction to him. Lily couldn't figure out why he forgot after meeting her each time. She'd seen some of the transport cops around him, but Jacob never noticed.

I wonder if he has been actively altering the lives of others, she wondered. *That would be the only reason he would be so carefully watched.* She decided to just go back home and plan her next adventure.

Chapter 9

The fragrance softly enveloped the atmosphere, causing Lily's eyes to open and peek at the new design of the day. She smelled new buds of fragrant spring rose petals and vibrant citrus blossoms. She breathed in, down to her toes, the freshness of the day. There was a hint of *him* in that smell, of his laughter, his smile, and skin and hair. The fragrance begged to hold her and sweep her away.

She wrapped herself in thought of pleasant and wonderful days of plenty, while imagining herself as Thumbelina in a bowl filled with petals that she pressed to her face, her skin absorbing every bit of their sweetness. He was calling her and she knew it. She remembered when they had traveled into time together and gotten lost. Lost in Paris in the wrong year. She had planned to see the Louvre when it was Louis XIV's palace, before he built Versailles. She had wanted to see the beginnings of this extravagance but they had traveled to 1988 instead of 1688. She wanted to see the French 'Great Culture,' and to dance with him in the palace.

They were 300 years late, but that was okay. She loved the right bank, and the Louvre as a museum, walking up the Champs Elysees, while cars and buses whizzed by, and the shops filled with much too costly clothing, and music pouring from the cafes and clubs. The type of music that made a person want to stop and just be there. You could even hold the music in your head and take it with you.

They walked under the Arc de Triomphe and identified the twelve streets that led into it. They found the Opera House; in fact, they circled it four times because she wanted to plant it all in her mind's eye so she'd never forget. They found a meadow filled with spring flowers, and Lily romped through them with her bare feet and laughed and owned another secret of real beauty. Jacob watched from a close distance, afraid to go near her and break her magical adventure.

The side streets were such fun with cooking visible through windows, then glimpses of succulent entries and pastries and scurrying and apples out front and the sound of running footsteps and catcalls that were really yells for attention. The sweet smell of freshly baked pastries grabbed her nose and taste buds and begged a real bite.

There was this street vendor with a dog and cat sleeping together in a basket; Jacob found five francs in his pocket to get her picture taken with them. At mid-afternoon, fatigue found them so they leaned against the jagged brown bricks, cooled their bodies and devoured each other with looks. They did not need to touch; their eyes caressed each other's souls. There was a door with just a single word on it and Lily wondered what was behind the door...it called her practically by name.

Jacob went into the building first and came out smiling, then took her hand and led her inside. It was a perfume house. He bought her the signature house fragrance in a little gold-colored metal bottle. She cherished it forever. The fragrance was spice and spring and vibrant citrus. She thought of his eyes whenever that aroma entered her space and saw him, she heard the sound of words but saw no form; he called to her and she answered.

Jacob tossed and turned while all around him was the hint of a girl he couldn't quite remember...her scent of fresh lemon blossoms and the perfume of lilacs surrounded him. How could he find her again? He imagined her eyes and they appeared before him. He knew she'd be in Egypt—there were clues left in his apartment and in his dreams—but he wondered if she'd want him there. He began his search for her, for the love of his life for pure unadulterated passion, something he knew she held for him alone.

Lily wondered about Jacob while she was not in his time, if his days were filled with wonder, excitement and laughter. For her, on some days there really were no reasons for why things happen the way they did. She sat on the top step outside her room and stared at the full moon marveling at its magnificence. There was no one to talk to and no one to listen, so the splendor of the moon kept her company.

She wondered if she could go back to the beginning of the moon's creation and see how it all began. Would that be possible, safe, or even within reason? Would Jacob want to know about the origins of the Earth and infancy, or think her foolish? Would he join her? Was she wrong in teaching him how to go with her through time and give him the gift of traveling? Was that a loss for her? Was his only interest now in undoing past wrongs of others throughout history?

She wondered if the consequences would be as severe as Professor Stevens had warned, if things were not left in their proper place when she left. She'd only taken a few tokens: a stone from the Sphinx and a pebble and a perfumed silk scarf from King Tut's tomb, a bottle of perfume in Paris and a snapshot taken in front of the Opera House with the sleeping cat and dog.

They called themselves the others or travelers to prevent being labeled anything unkind. So when Lily, Jacob and the others left the tomb she was wearing Selket's scarf and could only hold onto a pebble she'd taken because of Selket. Selket was still alive when she was placed there in the tomb with King Tut. She was put there to watch over his decaying body and saw her chance to escape so Selket tried to grab Lily as she exited, not to save her from harm, but so that she could leave the tomb, too.

The statue of Selket had been cast when she was a little girl. From birth her purpose was to watch over the King after his death. She had to accompany his rotting flesh and go with him to the life beyond, forever. Lily had to protect herself and try to protect Selket, knowing Selket would spend the rest of her days in this tomb watching the dead. Lily could not undo this reality.

When Selket saw Lily enter the tomb, she thought Lily was an angel or a goddess who had come to rescue her because of the way Lily materialized out of nowhere. From that moment, Lily was never out of her sight.

Lily decided to go to Egypt in the winter of 1323 BC because of the entries in Jacob's diary about the advanced civilizations of Egypt at this particular time. Also, he was trying to uncover the truth about Tut's death. She wanted to see their culture firsthand and how it compared to the 24th century AD. Since the days of the gray haze, when pollution had overtaken all areas of earth, her culture had been mostly stagnant.

The world turned out pretty much controlled with government taking over all individual freedom, yet it had happened years later than predicted, around 2200AD, it was. Even Kurt Vonnegets' book *Welcome to the Monkey House;* describes how human greed would forever damage the planet and individuals were not even allowed personal thought.

The haze began when people started to disregard the needs of the earth, using up too much of the resources at one time. Very little was left for the earth to use to replenish itself, as it should have been able to do. The earth was out of balance and all went haywire: horrific global storms, unstable weather patterns, and deformed births of almost all living things. A small remnant of the population and livestock remained whole. This meant that the food supply was also in peril. So people began to develop ways in which to leave the planet, again, in the process, unlocking the knowledge of time travel in the process. Oh, yes, it's always been a possibility! People would simply find a jump off point and leave the planet for a while.

When Lily first appeared Selket stood in amazement and felt no reason to flee from her. She reached out her hands to welcome Lily and to show her she, too, was safe and held no weapons. Lily was relieved as if a burden of pressure had been sucked from her spirit. Whenever she traveled and found that another human was present, she was frightened, because Kaye had gotten her out of some awful situations in the past. But in this instance fear left and Lily's goose bumped skin was smooth again. She allowed herself to take a deep breath and offer a smile.

The air held evidence of frankincense and myrrh, hyacinth and lilac. Lily knew that no matter where she traveled there were always spirits of goodness and angels, nearby. This was such a time.

Selket beckoned her to follow and she did. They entered what appeared to be a game room, sat and played a game much like checkers but with circular board moves. Lily laughed as she learned and found reason in the game. Selket spoke to her and the TTC immediately translated the words. "Why are you here? Have you come to take us with you? Have you come to select one of us? Who attends to your care? Is there one who takes care of you? Do you hunger? Thirst? Want?"

Lily realized that Selket believed she was a goddess or extraterrestrial, Lily was not going to tell her any different. The truth itself was unbelievable.

She stared into Selket's eyes and answered that she was there in search of knowledge. Their visual connection was electric, as if Selket had reached into the pit of her essence, and Lily allowed her entry. Selket's eyes were vacant as if her very spirit had been stolen, lost in tomorrow's search for reason. Selket understood without words. She led Lily into a room filled with tablets. As she touched each tablet, knowledge engulfed her—she learned of birth, death, time, space, distance, mathematics, astronomy, the soul, gods and goddesses, suns and stars, and planets. The last tablet was that of human spirit. She learned of its goodness and its wickedness. She held it close to her as fear fell from her face. Her mind was awakened and held a universe of thought within her.

Lily stood in the middle of the room surrounded by the tablets, stretched out her arms, palms facing up, and embraced the knowledge she'd received. She stood there for countless hours, her body soaking wet, while her old self was enervated.

With her palms facing the walls of tablets and fingers pointing to the ceiling, she began to revolve slowly as a cloud lifted and engulfed her. She'd accomplished one of her goals, even though only half of the tablets had been experienced. Selket led her back into the game room, and this time Lily understood the mind expansion these games offered. She played—not just to win, but to know how deep and how far she could go in her own mind, continuously finding solutions to others' moves. She wondered just how she could use these techniques in her everyday life: To know things. But there were more tablets her mind had to experience.

Other women approached them and one began to brush Lily's hair. Her hair was much like theirs but not as tight and wooly. They wanted to just touch her. Another removed her shoes and washed her feet, a tender, exalted benevolent washing as Lily continued to stare at Selket's eyes to continue talking without words. Dozens of women washed and massaged her hands, feet and head while another examined her shoes and touched her garments. Lily gestured that they should pamper Selket as well, and they did. She looked around as her vision became accustomed to the scant light and realized that food was there, preserved for years, and there were others caring for the bodies of the dead. They were all sealed in. But there was air; food and water, and private chambers; jewels and riches; and lovers for play and absolute imprisonment.

There were no doors…only corners and entrances, because there was no leaving. Lily was led to a chamber covered with the finest pastel silk and jewels. A portion of the floor fell away and a room-sized bath appeared. She felt compelled to walk forward and the women began to undress her. She had worn a wrist TTC for this trip and did not allow anyone to touch it. When one of them tried, she harshly scolded her shouting, "No." And they all stepped back in fear. That was the first time they'd actually heard her voice. Selket had told her while they played games that the attendants were waiting for their goddess, and they hoped that Lily was perhaps she. Their goddess was supposed to take them out of their prison and allow them to be free to live in a land of their choice.

It must have been a very special, significant place, because no one wore shoes in this fragrant room and they spoke only in whisper. The women touched her at first out of curiosity to see if she were real…flesh and blood. Then they bathed her in precious oils, perfumes and bubbly waters that seemed to spring from beneath her feet.

She saw blank expressions in their vacant eyes with smiles all around her and wallowed in their indulgence of her in this luxurious pampering. She was fan dried by women holding large colorful plumes, occasionally whisking her skin ever so slightly; almost inaudible sighs escaped from her throat as she remembered her very first full body massage, every part of her was relaxed and rejuvenated. The women massaged her muscles and draped her body in exquisite cloth. She wondered why there were no men there and Selket's mind told her that the men had their own chamber and they visited from time to time. However, the women were not allowed in their chambers other than to serve and entertain them. *Wow,* she thought. *Things haven't changed a great deal in all this time.*

Her eyes remained closed as she thought of Jacob and heard the sound of trickling water, and he was there.

Suddenly Jacob walked into the room and all the women scattered, having never before seen a male so tall and muscular. His heart leaped and when he saw Lily laying on a feather bed of lightly multicolored silk, and he realized this was the lady in his dreams. "Have you been waiting long?" he asked her.

She looked up into his eyes through her veiled coverings and smiled. She waited seconds longer to hold him captive, and replied, "All my life and longer."

Then, not of her own doing, she disappeared. Jacob had been within a whisper of touching her hand. He believed Lily wanted him to follow her and make this a part of his chase. He knew in her quest for knowledge and finding beginning of everything, she wanted to eventually find the Garden of Eden and decided where he would go. But he, too, was captured and vanished.

They were all there. Stevens, Hannah, Ben, and Cora were waiting. The four of them waited for loved ones to stream past so they could divert them to a safer landing. As the sound of liquid grew nearer and an essence raced through time, each and every cell transformed into basic elements, to catch up with its soul, they waited.

The four heard the rippling rivers and stood watching, hovering; so their next landing would be escorted to safety.

Ben took the lead this time ready with all systems ablaze for Kaye and Lily to return. Cora had his back because she knew there were others near. But the others had almost burned out all their times and truly believed that they could divert these three to their own calendars.

Kaye had almost reached Ben and Cora when a second stream crossed between them. When Cora reached for the steam just behind her, she realized that Lily was gone.

Jacob, with his hand still a breath away from Lily's, saw the vanishing and could not imagine what had just occurred. He knew she longed for him and vise versa, and wondered why she left so abruptly.

Jacob looked around and saw all the desperate souls, begging to leave the tomb. When the voices yelled, "You killed her!" he vanished, too.

Without waiting a second for the coast to be clear, PawPaw grabbed his stream as it entered his own realm. Jacob didn't have the opportunity to understand any of this. PawPaw took Jacob back to that very morning, minutes before he learned anything again about traveling.

When Stevens, Jacob's great-great-great-grandfather, joined the others they told him about Lily's kidnapping. Each tried in vain to recapture the second before and found that the seconds were gone. Again and again, their attempts were blocked.

They all looked to Stevens; and without outwardly uttering any thought, they each blamed the other. No one asked. They stood in their silent grief. Frozen hearts would not let them convey any messages of thought, and most of all hurt to each other. They did notice that Hannah was gone. But where?

Cora broke the ice saying, "She's an old soul and is excellent at taking care of herself and others."

"Can she tell us how to find Kaye and Lily?' Stevens almost begged.

"I hope she followed them so we can know at least they're safe and we can pick them up." Cora replied.

"Hannah's a strange little creature, don't you think?" said Stevens.

"Stop it!" Cora demanded. "She's always been here and she always will." Ya know, right when I stumbled into traveling, and began to understand it, this little girl appeared," Cora took a breath and waited a moment or two so that she could gather her thoughts back into her mind. "I tell you, she scared the hell out of me. Can you imagine?" Answering her own question, "Well, I couldn't!" she stopped for a moment and surveyed their surroundings.

"It's not safe here, lets meet at place #4 in Steven's Time." Said Ben.

"Which realm, man?" said Cora.

"How about #6?" Stevens chimed in.

"Deal?"

"Deal."

"Deal."

They scattered, knowing that Lily and Kaye were gone and Stevens had taken Jacob out of harm's way for the moment. Stevens missed Kaye and Lily by less than a second, but felt sure that Kaye had rescued Lily.

Chapter 10

Jacob had not believed in a lot of things before Lily crashed into his life. Lily actually reached in and rescued him away from the depression that engulfed him. She had saved him from the bad dreams and sleepless nights; back when it seemed like the best way to handle everything was to give up on life. Lily did not allow that to happen.

Now he believed almost anything was possible. He had never thought much about the future, but now knew that it existed and that people there in the future were actually watching over the present to make sure that the people in the present world did not destroy the world and it's set timeline. Jacob had come close to causing a paradox when he tried to find Grace. He went back to eavesdrop on their good times. But their times together were gone! Erased! As if she had never been.

He then decided he wanted to save his friend Baxter and he now had the ability, but it was not supposed to be. Those time robbers (he didn't know what else to call them), had shown up at the very last second, preventing him from doing what he'd wanted to do for at least 20 or so years. That was to stop the death of his close friend. The ordeal hurt a second time, and third and fourth, almost as much as it had the first time he tried. He could not bear to watch the scenario the fifth time and had pushed the "return" button before they could do anything about his being there again.

Jacob almost destroyed the house in anger upon his return. It was a week before he was able to even think straight about what took place. When he did think about it, all he wanted was to vent his revenge on them, any of them...the others. How dare they let his friend die! Who were they, anyway? Deep inside, he believed he knew who they were. He couldn't even explain it to himself, but he knew. The hurt dug at the pit of his core and made him ache like no pain he had ever felt. He cried until there was nothing left, and then shoved all those feelings so far inside that even he would not know where they were. It didn't make it any better that he knew who they were and felt the powerlessness of being unable to do anything about it.

Jacob knew now that he would definitely write the book— a copy of which Lily left on his doorstep. He would write about all the things that he'd seen and the places he'd been. People might not believe him but it didn't matter. He knew. He knew the truth. The truth of what really happened in so many incidents in history. His thirst for exposing the villains had been quenched, but only briefly. He had to find a way to get past the time robbers.

He was tempted to read the book and see what he'd written but decided against it. He did not want to influence himself in what must be written from the heart, but he would have to find a way to get back to his old self and write in peace. Jacob smiled to himself; it would all be from the heart. He did, of course, already know the title: *The Truth about History, First Hand*. At first Jacob wondered where he had gotten the title. But then he read through his original source research literature from his dissertation and discovered the title written sideways on a page of his notes, in his own handwriting. *When did I do this? He thought?*

He owed a lot to the students of his class. They'd given him ideas and locations of incidents. He made notes and used them to track his way through time and history in search of reason and truth.

His mind took him back around to the time when he first met Grace. She wore a black t-shirt, with big bold gold letters that spelled G.I.R.L., and underneath, if you got real close—which may have been the intent—it read "Goddess in Real Life." From the moment he saw her, he knew that to be true.

Jacob had been at a loss for words and stumbled upon an apology, asking her pardon for the clumsy accident. With the coy little half smile she said, "Ya know, there are no accidents." She didn't bother to explain that—for the moment. Those words that stuck in his mind.

He remembered when they'd sit for hours while he read to her. He especially like the poems of Rumi and so did she. Their favorite poem was in part:
"The minute I heard my first Love Story
I started looking for you, not knowing
How blind that was.
Lovers don't finally meet somewhere
They're in each other all along."
"Oh, she can't be gone" he cried out loud.

Chapter 11

A sign of relief escaped her, not that it was an unwanted chore or anything, but she'd completed their plan to meet so that she could tell him about how someone was tampering with his memory and they were going to set up a trap to find out who it was and why. She was never compulsive, not now anyway. She always wanted everything in its proper place, planned to the minute or to the second if that were possible. She'd been frivolous, carefree, nonchalant and wanton, most of her life because there had always been someone there for her to depend on who cared for her. But now, she wanted to grow on her own and make her own adventures.

Several years had gone by since her first attempt at time travel, and she and Kaye had since traveled through many times. They'd danced in a harem and served at Royal tables and rode bareback through the old west with Annie Oakley and sang songs on hilltops and met Perry and Henson at the top of Mt Everest. This is where their entourage thought that she and Kaye were angels.

She'd held hands with the slaves as she followed Harriet Tubman, marched with Dr. King in Selma, and covered her head to hear Malcolm, then sat quietly watching their burials. She went to the first moon launch and even comforted Sputnik. She could be anywhere at anytime and never lose a minute of herself. But her mind kept taking her back to that very first encounter. Who was Jacob? Why must she find him, and how? He was holding a piece of her and she, him. It was as if she'd been kissed on the lips by a desire that would not subside. Not an obsession, but a longing. Which was much sweeter.

On one of her trips she'd found a perfect piece of quartz the length of her feet and shaped like a small log, about a foot in diameter. She knew she shouldn't have, but she brought it back with her. She promised herself and Mother earth that she'd put it back in the same place at a later time. On the way back, it cracked in half and upon returning home she found it split in two pieces. The inside had a knotty surface and she made it into a footstool to massage the bottoms of her feet. For some reason it relaxed her to speculate, wonder and give way to the hope that she could find Jacob again. Like a little kitten presses its paws into earth's floor or a soft carpet, one after the other while quietly purring, she pressed her feet into the quartz footstool. She'd sit and read or daydream, trying to remove tangles in her thoughts.

Professor Stevens was at his usual spot, at the window facing east, when Lily approached his office. He was adjusting pieces of his machinery and gadgets and buttons and lights. "What's troubling you, young lady?" he asked when she entered the room. He sensed something pensive in her quiet manner, different from her usual self.

She smiled and walked around his space, inspecting his array of utensils and tools. She was silent.

"Am I to guess?" he inquired.

She looked at the floor and fingered an item on the table that was interesting. "What does this do?" she asked.

"Oh, just a project I'm trying to perfect," he answered.

"What will it do if it's perfected?"

"Some elements should never be allowed to come into contact with each other, and I'm developing a shield to ensure that."

"Oh," she said. "What if there are elements you want to be in contact. How can that happen?"

"Okay, Okay, what are you really asking me?" Dr. Stevens decided he needed to push for responses.

She dared not look at him but continued to inventory in her mind's eye all the equipment tabled there. She believed she had to remember all that was there and find out why it was. *There could be something right here that I'm looking at, something I need, and I have to figure out how to use it.* She thought

"Lily, hello..." Silence. "Are you there, Lily?" He pulled his eyeglasses down to the tip of his nose to peer at her more with his senses than his eyesight. *She is masking something,* he thought, but wouldn't dare ask.

She ran her fingers over the titles of his books in the shelf, then opened one and stared at the pages stark still until she found the words she needed to continue.

"What is it you came here to find, little girl?" his face remained expressionless. There was complete silence for almost four whole minutes. The air dried during that silence and she felt like her tongue had turned to cotton. Just dry. He waited.

It felt like hours to her, Lily examined her watch and immediately forgot what time she'd seen.

Her mind was racing elsewhere, outside the room, outside her realm. She didn't know quite how to phrase her query, and feared him thinking her terribly silly and naïve, or worse, an idiot. She had been called before, but not by him.

"Okay, okay, what elements would you like to see in contact with each other?" He finally asked. *I think that's what she's asking.*

Her frozen mouth attempted to form the words and finally broke open to say "Well," she began, "on my first try at time travel, I went alone and I encountered someone." She paused. "Someone who I'd like to find again."

Chapter 12

When Lily was abducted from Tut's tomb, Kaye had been the first one of the four to stand as a shield but she was also kidnapped as she was trying to prevent them from snatching Lily. So they found themselves in somewhat familiar surroundings but when they looked at each other they had both aged physically more than 50 years. Kaye reached out to touch Lily's face, and Lily told Kaye not to look at her own reflection.

"They got us, huh?" Kaye broke the silence.

"Yeah. What the hell happened?"

"Time thieves. When they grabbed us they also removed some of our existence."

"So we're going to just roll up and die like this? Lily hollered back as she stood in front of the full-length mirror. "Why didn't you tell me I could lose years if someone just decided to take mine? Can I go back?" Kaye held up her hand for Lily to stop talking, right there.

"No. We can't fight fire with fire. I know there must be another way," Kaye said as she sat rubbing her hands together and pulling back the wrinkled skin of her hands and forearm.

Lily turned to her and said, "There is a way we can re-program ourselves to get back and collect our stolen time." Said Lily.

"How?" asked Kaye in a pretty disgusted tone.

"Well, we have to first pinpoint a few things, then project into the future as well as the past." She began entering formulas into the TTC.

"How, pray tell, did you know that?" asked Kaye as her puzzled expression made her eyebrows meet in the middle of her forehead.

"Oh, I have to tell you what happened in the tomb after I met Selket."

"Oh yeah, and what's a Selket?"

"She lived there."

"And?" Kaye continued to prod.

"I found a pocket...no, a stream, she paused again. "No, an abundance of knowledge and learned how to relate critical thought to action." Said Lily.

"We have to know how to find each other when we track down the thieves." Said Lily

Kaye quickly rebutted Lily's last four words. "We don't want to track them down, we want to evade them until we are back to our wholeness, then we can send them to where they need to be."

"How will we know?" asked Lily.

"When the time is right everything will become clear."

"Yeah sure, and we will know exactly where we need to be?"

"Exactly!" she stopped and just stared at Lily.

"What else was in that tomb?" Kaye asked.

"We have lots of time to talk about that later. Right now I want to show you what we have to do, and we have to do it quickly." Lily went to work developing a formula for them to regain their time and escape.

They had to break lose from the hold Baxter and Tony had on them. Yes, Lily and Kaye saw them, they didn't know them but they recognize them as dangerous. Once free Kaye and Lily could recover their own time and begin the process to neutralize the thieves.

"So," said Kaye, "I ask again" a little louder this time, "what if one of us gets lost?"

"We will look for each other someplace where everyone needs to go."

"Where?" Kaye laughed, "the toilet?"

"Not a bad idea, but no. The grocery store, or any type store that sells food, fresh Produce." Lily answered.

"Okay, and do what, stand at the door?" said Kaye.

"No." picking up the grocery store receipt on the table near where they landed in the 1970s. Lily said "here," handing Kaye the piece of paper. "Lets look at two things on this list that you'd find never purposely put together. Let's say one perishable and one you could keep a while."

"I see a couple of things here that I couldn't imagine being on the same shelf." Said Kaye

"What?"

"Candy and vegetables."

"What's on that list then?"

"Strings beans…"

"Here, let me pick the other one…" Lily studied the list a minute. "Candy canes?"

"Yes, that works for me."

Lily looked at the TTC, braced herself and Kaye held on,…she pushed enter.

Lily fell backwards and continued to do so, while Kaye advanced further ahead. When they each landed, Lily was a little girl, a baby, and Kaye was well way past the age of survival on this planet.

Kaye remembered everything while Lily remembered nothing. Nothing because she was now a small child and could barely talk or understand language.

Kaye furiously searched all that was within her to find a way to get to Lily, because Lily had the travel instrument. As she walked past the mirror she realized that her body was older than it was a few minutes before. She checked her fingernails and eyes to try and understand how much she'd aged, figuring the same number of years aging may have been deducted from Lily's life.

Kaye believed her body's age was at least 98 years, so Lily must be 2 or 3 years old, if she wasn't wiped out altogether. She had to have been born, otherwise there'd be no years to alter.

Kaye began to search, knowing that their grocery store agreement was off for now. She did not have the TTC so she had to resort to out-of-body travel, which she hadn't attempted in years.

She regressed at five-year intervals and finally she was there, under the bridge a few blocks from where they'd been moments ago. Kaye took the baby

Lily home after finding the TTC had fallen from her arm and was on the ground leaning against the concrete wall. No one noticed it or Lily there in full view.

Kaye could still come and go, but she could repair neither her chronological age, nor Lily's. She realized that her body would soon expire and she placed Lily in the hands of friends who promised to care for her and upon Kaye's death they were to give her a sealed box.

When these friends used up the majority of the resources left by Kaye, they abandoned Lily. The next thing Lily knew, she was living in a foster home with nice people. She knew she didn't belong there. Lily was always seeing shadows of people, things, even places. Some places she saw several times in just a few minutes. Lily didn't know at the time, but her mind was trying to tell her who she really was.

One time she told her foster mother that she wanted to go outside to play with the little boy in her garden. The woman said, "There's no one out there...are you sleep walking again?"

Lily didn't mention the people she saw anymore. Only in her quiet space could she be who she was. When the shadow people came to talk to her, she'd answer or write them a note. The people at the foster home didn't understand her so they sent her away, too.

She knew she wasn't supposed to be there…but where was she supposed to be?

Lily grew up and began to mature and run into people who thought they knew her. The last place she lived before going off to college was with people who encouraged her and appeared to really want her to survive and succeed. They were strange people, sometimes they'd be sitting at the dinner table and one or two of them would disappear. But they didn't think that she was particularly strange so the relationship worked.

They guided her to a non descript College someplace west, near water. She then found herself in Professor Stevens' class. He knew who she was but was afraid to alarm her; he waited until she remembered anything that he could latch onto.

Chapter 13

Her statement pleased him immensely, because he knew that memories were coming back to her that he needed in order to try to undo the experiment Lily and Kaye concocted to escape the time snatchers the first time. How dangerous and *crazy that was*, he thought. They should have stayed put and their own group would have found them. When she spoke of the diaries her Aunt Kaye had left her, he was ecstatic.

The smile that engulfed him was only noticeable in his eyes and he was a bit fearful at the same time. He was not quite sure of what was being set into motion. His project, which was not yet completed, could keep things separated in time for as long as it was necessary. From Stevens' point of view, there were many more involved in the ghastly drama than anyone could have imagined. It was snowballing into an avalanche at that very moment.

If Jacob interfered with the death of his friend, Baxter, many people would die because there would be no outcry to stop damaging the atmosphere and pure time. Baxter left a notebook in his belongings that no one else really understood what it meant until Ben followed Candler after watching and listening to his conversation with Jacob about Vietnam. It was his plan to establish an entourage of angry travelers to help him siphon time from as many people as there were on earth, travelers or not. All the while their B-Team would remove massive amounts of natural resources with weather changes and other shifts in environmental placements of all living things to establish themselves as natural overpowering predators. They would control all chaos to their benefit and have power over all resources, natural and manufactured.

Many travelers knew of this B-Team but regarded them as idiots who had no understanding of what they were doing. So no one noticed until the damage had been set into motion and people began to die from catastrophic events, natural and Worldwide. Even the learned individual travelers were taken by surprise, and couldn't undo what had been set into this new reality. This B-Team blended into all times, groups and classes of people.

Everybody and everything else would be at risk. In essence, they would all live in abundance forever. Even though Baxter seemed insignificant, his realm included organizers, orators, statesmen, and leaders all obsessed with greed, and control who, when called for, would spring forward once Baxter was gone. He was actually picked to set this plan in motion, and to believe it was his master plan. But, only if Baxter was gone, and stayed gone in its early inception, could this drama be stopped? The powerful were not yet willing to be public with their plans and knew that the obsessive Baxter would go after whatever he could get done with reckless abandon and no one could point a finger at the real power brokers.

Those real powers did this not because of Baxter specifically but, by what he represented; youth, progress, the Black and White underground community, maleness, enterprise, greed, envy and cruelty. He believed he was fitting into a goldmine.

They even controlled the air for breathing and airwaves for all communication and travel. And, Baxter had no real exit plan for himself because he believed he was the one in control.

If Baxter lived, there would be an over abundance of greed and envy, coveting, blaspheming, murder and contempt because he would help destroy many souls with a carefree non-chalet 'I can live and do whatever I want forever' philosophy.

Professor Stevens knew that Baxter was out for revenge against anyone he ever felt harmed him or caused him any kind of grief during his tumultuous disaster of a childhood. It didn't have to be true, but if Baxter believed anyone had done something to him, it was so. Even the little girl who buried petals that he had given her. He believed he watched her destroy them, when all the while she was making them grow by planting them with the other flowers in her garden.

She would be first; after a time of grief for all around her, and those who knew her had time to heal, he could strike again. But for now Lily was his target.

"Professor, are you in there?" Lily interrupted his thoughts.

"Yes, yes, my dear, I just had to take pause to think of something I'm working on, and it came to me as you were walking into the room. I guess something you said jogged me right back into my project mode, "

"I'm sorry I interrupted you. I'll come back later." She said.

"No, no please stay. I want to know more about the diaries your aunt left you. She sounds like a fascinating women."

"I don't remember too much about her personally, just mostly what people said and how she'd ramble on about past events. She could tell great stories. But you know, every once in a while—I don't know if I'm daydreaming or what but she kind of...appears and tells me things and leaves. "

"When does this happen? I mean, under what circumstances?"

"Well, I'm usually alone, but that's the only common denominator."

"Tell me, and I hope I'm not causing you any grief with this, but when did she...pass away?"

"About when I was 10." She looked at the floor and then the edges of the table.

"Do you have any other family?"

"No, no one, but the last people I lived with were pretty cool. I go to see them from time to time, and I keep picking up things that they saved for me.

That's when I first got those diaries I told you about. They, the diaries that is, are kind of weird. She was a scientist, you know."

"Yes, yes, you told me that."

"I've been trying to figure out some of the formulas written in them but they don't make a lot of sense. I mean some are formulas that have an almost infinite, absolute power. Can you imagine that?"

"No, maybe one day you could share some of her writing and we could figure out what she is saying in regular, everyday terms.

"Sure. How about next Thursday?"

"That will be fine, young lady." Lily turned to leave. As she reached for the doorknob, she heard water rushing but didn't stop because she'd heard that before near the door. She got a little chill each time she heard it. *I am supposed to understand what that sound means,* she thought. And just as quickly, the sound and the thought of the sound disappeared.

Chapter 14

In Lily's miscalculation of time and place, nothing greeted her except quiet. An evil, sterile, eerie quiet. The kind of quiet that made her listen for the creaking sound of a sneaky footstep or the slow hollow edginess on the un-oiled door hinge. This was the kind of quiet where she'd hold her breath to maintain the silence and try to continue to hold it in. To embrace her own fear she wrapped herself in the dare so she didn't run; but should she? Her skin turned cold and felt almost damp, she couldn't tell if she were chilled or sweating. Her head told her to go back but her heart and soul bade her wait and stay still. None of her muscles moved for what felt like forever, not even her eyes. Tiny lights flashed all around her dining room table as she sat in front of her bowl of cereal and held her spoon midway from the bowl to her mouth. She sensed the flashes of light before she actually saw them, not moving her eyes from the spoon.

Now just on the other side of time, she heard a tiny red raspberry of a purr, from a cat, breaking the silence. A small domestic cat stared at her with approval. He slowly stepped over to her and rubbed his body against her shoe. She remained frozen. He danced on both her feet and played with her laces, then settled and pushed his front paws one at a time into her shoes, continuing his purr.

There was a sadness in this dwelling and she could not tell why or what. She took a deep breath and found no scent of spice, or herbs, or flower, food or even decay. Sterile! She heard a stir in the other room. She shouldn't have come here, but she couldn't stay away either. She had to see him, if only in a quick glimpse. Ever since Professor Stevens told her that he had a grandson, an obsession overtook her. Lily had to see, touch, smell and hear his very essence. She still could not identify the connection between them.

She remembered how the Professor had told her Jacob was not to learn of travel because his heart would lead him to create havoc. Not that Jacob was unkind; on the contrary, he wanted to undo wrongs that were not his to undo. Stevens told Lily of their first encounter in a collision while traveling through time. Lily understood the bracelet. He asked that she not disturb anything but could observe as much as she wanted. She promised she wouldn't touch anything, or even consider taking any little trophies, although she wanted to leave his bracelet and take her gold chain. She did not.

Jacob entered the violated space and Lily saw him. He walked, head down, drowsily, through her space and into another room. She placed her hand over her heart, which was pounding as if her body surrounded a drum in full orchestra.

He was not at all 'the person' she ever thought he'd be. The picture that danced in her mind was not the man she'd just seen covered only from the waist down, in pajama bottoms and bare feet. His satin brown skin brought thoughts of purest honey to her mind, his shoulders were broad but drooped in sadness and he had a bit of stubble with the beginnings of fresh beard and a head of wool.

He walked past her without looking up or sensing her presence. Her eyes were fixed on his countenance as the cat tiptoed behind him. He retrieved a small bowl from the floor and rinsed over it in the turquoise sink that was way too short for him. He added some sort of mush from a can then filled another bowl with milk from the fridge. She marveled at the strength of his stature. He stood up and turned around suddenly and looked at her eyes. She was caught in his gaze for one tiny second, then realizing she'd stayed too long, she pressed enter and vanished.

When she arrived home after that impromptu visit, her mind took her to all she'd seen in his home. There were pictures on the table next to her, and the images of some of them seemed familiar. There was also a diary, maps and messy notes written around the edges of typed pages. Little yellow flowers were in one of the pictures, buttercups maybe. She sat for what could have been a lifetime and found the little girl that lived inside her and searched her mind. This collection of things was supposed to mean something to her and she was desperately trying to find it. Memories whirled around her like ocean sprays and light rays at precisely 10 minutes past sunrise. That was the time that her spirit was fully engaged because that was the time of her physical birth. She went to go back and examine those pictures. She thought she even saw a likeness of herself in one of them. But she didn't go because the room felt dangerous.

There was a sinister feeling in the air, as though a cherished belief would prove folly or worse. She thought *that perhaps some sort of life threatening danger hung nearby.*

The little boy? She thought, I wonder if there are answers in him? Why did I remember a little boy all of a sudden?

Professor stood across the room, "what's got you troubled dear?" he said without ever looking up at her.

"There is something I'm supposed to remember and my mind won't tell me."

"How does it make you feel?"

"I'm not sure. It's like there's something I cherish, ya know, something I believe is suddenly no longer true, or has never been true, and all this time I thought it was. I wonder why I didn't see the difference before. I'm missing something that's right before my eyes, and I don't know what it is I'm supposed to see."

"Is it here, now?" he asked

"It's inside me somewhere, but the key is elsewhere. I don't know if it's an idea or object, a person, a lover or dear friend. An important part of me is anguished, for whatever reason I'm not sure."

"You say you're missing something?"

"Yes, I lost something along my journeys either this last one or one of the others' times."

She searched the air for a sign. Anything. Then she remembered that there used to be shadows and they weren't there anymore. They just stopped appearing. Just then the air released a "ting" as if from a chime. She turned in its direction, but there was nothing.

"Did you hear that?" she asked

"Hear what?"

"Like a weird chime."

His eyes widened "A chime?" he echoed.

"Yes, just one. You must have heard it."

"I can't say I did, but that's not to say there wasn't a sound."

"So you want to patronize me now, huh?"

"Oh no, no, no dear. If I sound that way I don't mean to be. I apologize if I sound condescending. I understand everything you've said to me. It's just that I'm trying to help you find that place in your mind for you to know what you must know." He did seem more interested in what she was saying once the chime was mentioned.

"Almost all my life I've seemed to be a bit out of step with everyone else." She paused. "Don't laugh, I see that 'uh huh' smile of yours."

"Now you are reading something that's not coming from me, child."

"I'm not a child" she stamped both feet, one then the other into the hard wood floor and her hand pounded on the desktop.

Professor backed his shoulders away and with his head cocked to the right breathed out a questioning, "ok?"

Professor Stevens dared not go closer and let the silence linger; then linger more. He stared at the space just above her hair, and watched her aura begin softening into calm.

"How in the hell did she do that?" He dared not ask. The bright amber glow around her head vanished and became a quiet miniscule glow from within her.

The resounding quiet of the room welcomed the patter of foot traffic on the path below the third floor corner window at the farthest point in the room from him.

Her head turned to a sound she heard over her right shoulder as her eyes left the curled into a soft fist of fingers, which now quickly opened to brace her against the desk. The "ting" from the window held her attention along with the swift air swish just behind her ear.

"I wonder a lot, why people see me and think or act as if they think I know more than I really do?"

Her conversation with the professor was aimed toward the window. He looked where she was staring and saw nothing unusual.

"Well," he said, "We all know how very smart you are and we don't think you realize it, the strength, I mean in what you know. Then too, we all want the best for your future." She began to speak, but he held up his hand halting any sound from her. "I've spoken to your parents, I mean grandparents, well, foster grandparents, and they are very hopeful for you to continue their legacy."

"What legacy?" she asked as the room went stark cold quiet, again.

Professor coughed almost to the point of choking and Lily picked up a cup of water to hand him.

"Are you alright?" she asked.

He continued to cough even harder. She walked him to a chair and filled his cup again. She stood there looking at him as her right eyebrow rose without effort. *I guess I'd better let that question alone for now,* she thought.

Professor sucked air in with clenched teeth, thinking *"What Pandora's box did I just open?"*

"You know, where I just came from...?" Was left hanging in the air. "...there were these diaries there." She said.

"Diaries, where?"

"At Jacob's house. I don't think he's read them any, at least not recently because they're dirty and haven't been touched in months, maybe years."

He gave her that "go on" kind of look.

"Well they look like they're just on display or something like you see in those old dusky museums or vintage kind of shops."

"They're just there at one end of each shelf...it's odd they aren't all together, but on different ends of the shelves."

Professor became much more restless. "Could you tell what they looked like? I mean color, fabric, size and such?" He caught himself becoming overzealous and did not want his sudden curiosity to alarm her. His cough was forgotten. He needed her to remember more about the shadows and the people who came with her.

Chapter 15

Lily was called Gnocchi, by those who loved her. The word meant; tiny dumpling. Especially those who wanted her to stay in place with their aspirations for her future. She rebelled and began to scratch out her own life. A life of exploration, intrigue and search and picking things apart is what she wanted. There was an answer for her, her quest for "place." She just knew it. The 'whisper' of an eyelash symbol that curved slightly at the top like a question mark behind her right ankle compelled her to search for the pattern of its meaning. Her meaning. There was an aura about the symbol that said, "understand your Times." She questioned that now, because it didn't say 'time' it said 'Times.'

She had known quiet voices and shadows, but they vanished when she grew out of childhood. It was as if she was caught in a doorway between dimensions. She was not being pulled in two directions, but rather both of them forged ahead into her being as a confluence of her total self, like two rivers merging.

The earth held a truth for her, and when she chose to study science, physics in particular, and later anthropology, at the university, all were puzzled. "Lily? " she heard from the other room. "Lily, are you going to join us? You know we've all been waiting for your homecoming and…your music is lovely dear, but come talk to us."

They were all there, this time, for her third graduation. No one called her Gnocchi anymore; since Aunt Kaye was more or less gone, now only he did, the little boy who brought her flowers.

She folded the cloth she'd been using to polish the wood of her cello. He had been her friend for as long as she could remember any thought at all. She called him "Cob" and she touched that tiny space while her fingers lingered at the 'whisper' she etched on his side so long ago. She remembered his hands as they scratched the message to each other with sticks on their skin. He had the same mark on him that she had. He stopped coming to see her and she didn't know where to look for him. The last time he visited her, he brought her, a bag full of flowers. He knew she liked yellow so he picked a bunch of yellow petals. They looked yummy, but when she tasted them they were nasty and burned her mouth like bitter weeds.

When he left, she took them outside to the burial ground she made for all of her pets. It was funny that every year, no matter what had been done to the soil there, the little yellow flowers poked their heads out each spring and stayed through summer and almost through the winter. Even though the taste was ugly, she tasted one of the petals every year just to help her remember how it was to be with her friend. Her face crinkled and anyone could see the gritting of her teeth as the taste set off the sour watery glands in her mouth and throat. The last time she saw him she could not have been more than six years old.

There was also another little boy who often watched Cob and Gnocchi play. He wanted to play with them a time or two but they didn't notice him and he never joined in. Mostly, he lurked in the shadows. He brought gifts and left them for Gnocchi on her favorite back step. Bax saw how much fun they seemed to have with the yellow petals, so he found some petals that looked exactly the same and handed them to her one day. Then later that day he saw her bury the petals in her little graveyard and he felt she was burying him.

Saddened that his gift was rejected he said nothing and just watched from a distance. That tiny kernel of rejection stuck in his throat, for always but she never knew.

The party had begun in celebration of Lily's latest graduation. She joined them, her family and the others and listened to their tales, and combed the room with majestic, mysterious; elegant eyes for a 'window'...her place for escape. She didn't know why, she just knew it was there.

They noticed as she graced the room. She had an inner royal beauty worn glowingly. There were no words for it, it just was—an essence of something precious, so they held onto her without permission. Her innocence mystique concealed the knowledge of how she looked from their understanding. Folks couldn't help but love her and want to be in her life if only for a short stay...her goodness was her royalty? It seemed that she really wasn't a part of this celebration at all, it was just in her name.

She wore purple and green and different patterns and textures, and it went together even though it wasn't supposed to. Black mostly was the foundation for all her lively colors, though there was always a hint someplace of yellow. Her dark brown hair "good hair" it was called in some of the times she visited, was pulled back always into a bun wrapped with ribbon, revealed dark golden brown skin, enchanting eyes and perfect facial bones.

Again, Lily tried to reach Cob with her mind. No answer.

Five years prior, a computer foul up placed her in Professor Stevens' class, physiognomy. His eyes, widened and Lily could read his astonishment, joy, sadness and pain in one quick glance. A zap of energy engulfed her and left just as quickly. No one else noticed that glance and neither acknowledged it to the other.

Graciously or selfishly, Stevens took her under his wing and she became his prize pupil. He re-introduced her to playing music not just holding onto the cello.

"Just this most recent summer," he said to his friends Ben and Cora, "I was ready to give up finding my old friend, Comrade and Traveling Bud, he called her. He felt there was great promise in Lily's character and intelligence. She was often challenged with much more advanced projects than her classmates and she aced them all. *She could lead him to his best friend and the others.* He knew that.

Professor's thoughts of what lead to this very moment evaporated as his mind brought him back to the present in the classroom, standing there with Lily Miller.

He had to find another way to bring the others out of hiding, captured or being unknowingly lost. Lily was the only one he'd discovered. But she had no idea who she was or where she really came from. He'd met the ones who adopted Lily but they didn't know the extent of her powers, nor did Lily fully understand them.

It was odd that the Professor had traveled back to the time of his first generation of grandchildren and found Jacob. There had to be a way for him to put the two of them together. But first he had to test the possible outcome.

Since the two of them have met before, he thought, *there's already a connection.*

"Professor? Hey are you up there?" She brought him back to the proper moment. "You were really lost, in thought. I thought you'd gotten lost or left the planet or something, you had a weird look on your face"

"Oh, we've all more or less been misplaced from time to time, perhaps another planet was with me."

"Ok, I'll see you next week." *What an odd statement*, she thought. *But, then too, he was an odd statement.*

"Don't forget your paper is due."

"Oh, its finished already, remember, we talked about that?"

"Yes, yes, of course. So that leaves you with no work to do?"

"I'm making a rug for my new apartment"

"Oh, your folks finally allowed you to move out on your own?"

"Professor, I've been on my own really all my life. They just keep tabs on me." She laughed on her way out through the main door.

"Bye."

He waved after her back was turned to leave.

Halfway down the hall she realized that the bag with her latch hook needles was still on the desk so she went back but no one was there when she opened the door and she'd seen no one in the hall. *I wonder where he went that fast?* She lowered her head to look around mysteriously, questionably, then picked up her stuff and left.

How strange, she thought

***

In that same second more than two hundred years earlier..."Hey, PawPaw, how've you been? I wasn't expecting anyone but come on in, the place is a mess."

PawPaw grabbed Jacob by the arms and hugged him tight. "My son, how are you doing? I'm just passing though and thought I'd pop in to see what you are up to."

"PawPaw, I've been teaching since I got back from the war. I'm trying to get the school to accept my programs and classes I'm interested in teaching."

"You will, son, you'll get whatever you want if you stick with it. Or if you decide early enough you want something else, go for that, too."

"Boy, when are you gonna find yourself a wife? I thought for sure you'd be married with at least two or three little rug rats by now."

"Aww man, I'm not ready for all that, yet. The girl of my dreams just hasn't run into me yet. I bet she's trying to find me at this very second."

PawPaw laughed from deep inside, "maybe so, maybe so." Knowing full well she was.

"Let me go make up the spare room for you. I'll get the clean sheets and pillows...you need anything else?"

"You got some bourbon or scotch?"

"Well now, I think I can help you out with that. Yeah, I can fix us something after I get your room done, or just help yourself." Jacob hollered from the back room.

PawPaw went to Jacob's room to look at the bookshelf. "No diaries," he said out loud.

"Did you say something, PawPaw? What are you doing in here? This is just my old junky room. Here, let me get you a drink so you can relax. Where are you coming from this time?"

PawPaw swung around not expecting him to be so close. "Oh, I was just casing the joint the way you used to do mine before you ran off to school."

"Now you know that's not so."

"You want me to give you the dates and times? You always rummaged through my things. Turnaround is fair play." PawPaw laughed even more. "Get me that drink! I'm only going to be here one night, I have work to do but I thought about you and since I was so close I wanted to see how you are doing."

He stalled looking around Jacob's room. "I know war can be hell, and I don't see that you're doing much for fun."

"I go out once in a while. But I've got so much I need to do before I get all involved with a lady."

"You better watch out boy, you'll let the good ones pass you by."

"No, I want to do the choosing, but not until I'm ready."

"First you better clean this place up, 'cause you bring someone into this dump like it is, she's gonna run out of here, quick."

They clicked their glasses high and laughter drifted off into far away glances that paused at different parts of the room.

"You know, PawPaw, I can't stop but think that she's just around every corner I turn, and our paths will cross soon." He cleared his throat to gather his thoughts. "She'll want to share her life with me forever. I'm not going to be like everyone else, you know, in and out of relationships, in and out of drug stupors and with no real direction…I want to be committed and I want to be ready for that."

"Hold it, hold it!" PawPaw held up his hand to halt the Mr. Nice Guy bullshit he had just heard. "I was not born yesterday. What's the real story?"

Jacob took a long drink, and a deep breath. "I can't shake what I saw in Vietnam. I don't sleep because my dreams take me back there and…" His voice wandered off to a whisper. "I can't talk about this."

"I'm here if you want to talk, but I won't pressure you to. A three swallow pause, watched them staring at their dreams, even full story epics of their lives that they couldn't share.

PawPaw's imitated slur broke the silence. "You know, you are so strong and ya don't need anybody…well that's fine, but ya know, I raised you from a pup man, didn't I?" PawPaw looked Jacob in the eye and he could see why the voices in his head had told him that Jacob needed him there.

Jacob starred at the pattern in the tablecloth, an odd set of squiggles that looked like a bunch of string beans and question marks. He'd never noticed it before. He only bought it because it was red and green and he was going to have a Christmas party a few months ago.

"Yeah, this table cloth has to go!" PawPaw said and they laughed and looked at the almost-empty bottle.

"How did you know what I was thinking? You used to do that to me all the time."

"Well, you were tracing the damn string bean with your finger, that didn't even take a guess." Each wrapped himself in an inebriated cloak to bring the conversation to a welcomed close for the night.

"Let's turn in. Your bed is made, and I'll get up to start some coffee in the morning. What do you want for breakfast?"

"To know that you had a good night's sleep."

"Night PawPaw,"

"Night, son"

Few words were spoken for the rest of the visit, which lasted a month, quite a bit longer than first announced. Jacob slept well at night and when he left for work each day, PawPaw either traveled to different times or continued to search the house for clues of the diaries.

I must go to a different Time, or dimension to find them. But how had she seen them? He wondered.

During breakfast the first morning, Jacob did tell him that he had a friend who was killed on one of their assignments and Jacob felt partially responsible and when he said his name, PawPaw shivered and asked him "You and Baxter went to grade school together didn't you?"

PawPaw inconspicuously grabbed the bottom of the chair with both hands to mask the tension in his face. PawPaw now knew who had to be responsible for the disappearance of so many in his circle. *The key is in this house!* Thought PawPaw, whom Lily knew as Professor. *But what Time is it in, whose realm?*

"Its just a little after 7:00AM, did I wake you up too early?

"Oh, I'm just speculating out loud, trying to remember an appointment." PawPaw chuckled under his breath. "I catch myself talking out loud. I guess its age."

On the 30th day, he wrote a "see ya later" note to Jacob saying, "I'll come back at another time." And left.

Chapter 16

His mind was miles away in Vietnam in 1970. Jacob heard the sounds of a fire mission conducted by the heavy artillery unit located over the hill. They were to cover their patrol area for the next four days. The sounds of the guns in the distance were constant for almost an hour. Jacob had become so accustomed to hearing them, that when they stopped, it was almost five minutes before he realized what was bothering him was that he was not hearing the guns anymore. He felt anxious, waiting for the next round to go off. His mouth was dry with the taste of dusty air. He counted in his head, and reached seventy-five when the artillery started again. For some reason he felt safe then.

The little lights on the floor flickered again and Jacob turned quickly to see the mouse running past. He watched now, every time the light flickered, he saw the mouse running from his spot of safety to some unknown area where food had been left. As Jacob breathed deeply and as he inhaled the night air, he smelled the cigarette smoke as Cook and Chambers were still jabbering away. He smelled the freshness of the ground after a day of rain.

The last sounds he heard before he fell asleep that night, were the guns. Then the sun came up and warmed the earth and made it all seem like new. Faint fragrances of sweet flowers, he did not recognize filled in the air and it all seemed so peaceful. Just at that moment he knew what a breath of fresh air felt like. Is *there really a war going on here?* Ran though his mind.

At 0530 hours Jacob was standing with his troop near the helipad. Everyone checked their gear making sure they had everything and nothing rattled. Commander Bill Donner, and the platoon sergeant came up and conducted pre-flight departure inspection. Each man jumped up, anything that rattled was taped down. Anything that shined was covered with black tape or tucked inside, loose gear was taped down. Bill and the sergeant were satisfied and they departed for the Valley. It was 0600.

Coming back to the present, Jacob cleared his head, looked around and shook off a cold chill. He had been sitting and thinking for over an hour. He hadn't thought about Vietnam or Baxter in a long time; nor remembered clearly the events of that last patrol. He went to the bar in his den, and poured a drink, downed it quickly and poured another. The smell and taste of Southern Comfort went straight to his head.

He wrinkled his brow, allowing the warmth to settle in his stomach. He walked back to the couch and allowed his mind to re-visit Vietnam, again and again and again.

The helicopter made three attempts then set down on a small hill covered with tall elephant grass. The team members leapt out the helicopters into a defensive position and waited for the copters to leave. Jacob's platoon remained still, long enough to hear and sense their surroundings. Then Commander Donner gave the signal to move out.

The men were to approach the edge of the elephant grass just below a ridge and follow it to a lip that looked down into the jungle. They moved quickly and quietly most of the day, careful not to follow any observable trail. They did not want to invite disaster.

The move into the valley had been uneventful, but there was one disturbing sign as they neared a small streamed.

There were what appeared to be pig tracks at the pool and overlapping some of the tracks were the huge tracks of a cat, obviously a tiger. Tension among the team increased. The point man, Jackson, spotted the tracks and upon checking the size, had spread his hand and fingers wide and his hand had not completely covered the paw size of the track. The cat was huge. After seeing the tracks, everyone got sharper on observing everything.

There was a small knoll that looked down onto a trail, they checked it and determined that there had been a lot of activity here at some point. They were to take a site just below the knoll and be prepared to watch the trail the next day.

As they moved into the harbor, they made a kind of hook turn into position to be sure no one was following. But then, walking backwards half the time was the job of the last man in the patrol to make sure that no one was following.

They moved in to set up for the night. Every man was within eight feet of another. Donner looked at Jacob and asked, "OK, buddy, you think you can set up the traps on the south side?" Jacob nodded. Donner then looked at Chambers. "Chambers you set the north side traps, Donald, you set the south side. Do it." "Cookie, you come with me and set the decoys.

Doc set the decoys for Chambers. There were five different settings of sensitivity on the transmitters indicating different types of intrusion from heavy vehicles to individuals. Each transmitter had a unique signal. Any intruder who set off a second sound was in the kill zone. This kept the site safe while everyone except the watch team rested.

Jacob crawled fifty feet with Doc close behind. As he set up the traps, Doc set up the decoys and they covered the wires, working their way back to the site. No words were spoken during this operation.

Jacob worked with the traps during the training and knew he was proficient at setting them up right. Neither man noticed Doc catch his foot on the wire and pull the connection loose from one of the transmitters. Doc released the wire from his boot and started to crawl behind Jacob when there was a sound of movement coming from behind. Jacob and Doc stopped immediately and stared back in the direction from which they came. Suddenly there was another sound, like air being sucked into a vacuum. They waited and watched. Nothing else moved. Doc looked at Jacob and pointed in the direction of the site.

Jacob and Doc crawled toward the sound. They had only moved a short distance when Jacob stopped and pointed a finger to his nose indicating that he wanted Doc to smell the air. The odor was strong now and Jacob looked around to see if he could determine from which way it was coming. It seemed stronger to his right, Jacob crawled through the high grass and put his hands down in something wet on the ground. Blood. The wetness on his hand made him shiver. The combination of the sticky, blood and the stench was almost more than Jacob could stand. He grabbed a handful of dirt and washed his hands to get rid of the sticky red stuff.

Without thinking, Jacob took the safety off his weapon. The stench was so strong and he wanted to vomit. *Later,* he thought. He parted the grass and saw the carcass of a dead pig, its guts spilled and ripped apart. Its' hind legs had been eaten off and so had one of the front shoulders. Now what got his attention he though, *what made the kill?* He looked back at Doc and they both understood. Jacob mouthed the word, "Tiger.

"They back tracked away from the kill and made their way back to the site, laying out the wires for the traps and decoys as they went. When they arrived, Donner asked. "what kept you?" Doc nodding his head back, as Jacob told him.

"Doc spotted a Tiger kill not more than 50 yards from here." Everyone sat up immediately.

The fear on everyone's face was apparent. All of them were shaken by the activities of just getting settled into the site, no one thought much about the tiger tracks seen at the water hole earlier. Now it all came rushing back too clearly to Jacob's mind. He thought, *the size of the tracks meant the cat was huge and close by. Had they scared him off his kill?*

They knew the tiger was still in the area. But was he still hungry? Everyone's face in the platoon reflected the same questions. "Was he still hungry?"

Donner sat silent for a few seconds going over the situation in his head. He then looked at Doc, Cook and Chambers and asked, "Did you guys get the traps set up with decoys? If you did it right, that cat couldn't get in here without us knowing it. If he does, we will blow his stripped ass back into the jungle. We will be safe as long as the radio watch is awake and on his job."

"Cook, assign the radio watch as soon as you and Chambers finish setting up the rest of the traps." Said Donner.

Jacob reported to Donner that he was not getting a signal from the second transmitter. He had tested the sensitivity several times. "You either crossed the terminals or you left a loose connection...and you know what that means?" Everyone looked at Jacob; Jacob looked back at all the faces and then at Baxter.

Without saying a word he picked up his rifle and turned to start crawling in the direction of the traps.

Baxter grabbed his gear as he started to crawl away and pulled Jacob back. "You stay put." Baxter grabbed his rifle, looked once again at everyone and crawled off into the bush.

Doc crawled over to Jacob and said, "Don't worry about Baxter, he's ok, he's just trying to play the hero and take care of all of us, he'll be alright, soon as he gets back, you'll see." Doc was really reassuring himself, his insides were raw with worry about what Bax was crawling into. Jacob looked at Doc and then turned to look in the direction that Baxter crawled. Everyone's senses were keened and honed, listening and watching into the darkness, smelling the air for any sign of danger. It had only been about three minutes but it seemed much longer. Jacob's stomach was turning over and over and with each turn getting tighter. He heard something like a shot, but it wasn't, it was voices, they could definitely hear what sounded like muffled voices and then it happened. They heard a loud awful blood curdling sounding yell that went on like the clanging gong at the strike of a clock on any chilling midnight. Baxter's screams broke the night air, followed by the roar of the tiger. Baxter screamed once more then there were no sounds other than the rustling of the brush.

Everyone grabbed their weapons and ran in the direction of the screams, throwing caution to the wind. As they reached the area, a sound of sucking air and rushing water could be heard. Everyone stopped. They moved fast and reached the traps, then spread out looking for Baxter. Chambers whispered, "Over here." The grass was flattened and a blood trail led into the direction of the jungle. In the middle of all this, lay Baxter's rifle. What was left of his right arm still clutched the stock of the weapon. No one moved.

They waited a few minutes for what seemed like days and decided that they would move out now and not wait for morning.

Jacob's spirit was dying inside. He felt as though he had been shot in the heart. Baxter was dead and it was his fault. He had caused his friend's death by not paying attention to what he was supposed to be doing. He thought about how he had set up the traps and remembered attaching all the wires and double-checking each one afterwards.

Jacob awakened to the memory of the feeling, not of Vietnam but...crushed flowers. He didn't even remember who crushed and buried them. He just remembered they were golden and living and touchable and he had watched them grow. He almost felt tears welling up around his right eye. Tears from years of wondering what had happened and could not understand why, it was just a feeling, his child within feeling.

It takes so little to crush a human spirit. The spirit surrounds itself with an impervious shield to keep anything else from causing pain, again. Little does it realize that it is also holding onto the injured spaces, keeping them injured. Jacob had such a feeling when the thought of his friend Baxter's death entered his mind. His spirit haunted him, too. Jacob was compelled to undo his death. He sat up, shivering and soaking wet, out of what he though was a deep sleep.

"That was that 'Nam' dream again." He surprised himself when he realized it was his own voice. "Damn!"

Shadow sat, head turned to the side, looking at him, then licked his paws as if to say, "Ok, feed me, now."

Chapter 17

Jacob aimlessly walked barefooted to the kitchen and took out the carton of milk and a can of Shadow's food. He froze when he heard a sound in the other room; a blurred someone walked past the doorway. Then the house felt normal again and his mind went back to 'Nam for the whole scenario—months he thought—but actually only seconds had passed.

His thoughts brought him back to the present again, so Jacob walked to the liquor cabinet, quickly opened the Southern Comfort and poured himself a healthy drink, downed it quickly and poured another. With the bottle in one hand and the glass in the other, he paced the length of the house. His mind ran rampant over the events of the past. Had he actually witnessed Baxter's death, again; and was it his fault?

He drank directly from the bottle now even though he still carried the glass as he slowly paced back and forth across the room. He thought about his life and how it had come down to these nightmares and when he had an opportunity to do something.... *Wait a minute*, he thought. Something nagged at him. He stopped in the middle of the floor with the bottle paused for another drink and froze like a snap shot. It came to him. He saw it. Cook's foot had pulled the wire loose. He had set the wires right on the traps. Cook's foot got tangled up in the wire and pulled it loose. Holding his head, covering

STRING BEANS & CANDY CANES

both ears, he replayed the event again in his thoughts. He slowly lowered the bottle as he continued to walk across the floor in slow motion. Staring down as if he could converse with the floorboards, he thought that he needed to talk with someone...But all those guys from the platoon were scattered who-knew-where. Picking up the bottle again, he watched the golden liquid swirl in the bottom of the glass. Time didn't move. Nothing did; his head was trapped in that far away nightmare.

Jacob stopped and set the glass and bottle down. He then stood at the bar looking at the glass shelves with different size glasses. His image peered back at him from the wall mirror. He saw streaked camouflage paint and a sweaty face staring back at him. No matter what he thought, he still came up with the same answer, the answer he had been looking for in the bottom of a bottle for over 20 years. The more he now thought about it, the better he felt. It was as if the weight of a thousand mistakes were lifted from his shoulders.

He stared back at the image in the mirror and said out loud, "You did not cause Bax's death." He said it again and again and each time he believed himself more. "You did not cause your buddy's death. You did not cause his death." He reached for the bottle and didn't take a drink this time in celebration for realizing the truth. He capped it and closed it up in the cabinet.

Jacob began to pace again. There were questions to be answered and thinking to be done and then he remembered there were others there...*Who the hell were those guys in the funny looking cloths?* Why....Were they there? Jacob was waiting for the tiger and would have had an easy shot when those guys showed up.

It was obvious to Jacob that the men were not from 1967, but when were they from? They must have come there to stop him from changing things. They were there to stop a paradox. Jacob now wondered, what *would have happened? Could the world not survive with such a minor change?* Evidently these guys had been sent there to stop him before he made that paradox occur.

Jacob remembered talking with one of the science professors some months ago about that very subject. It had been the professor's opinion that changing the past or preventing a paradox was like a very sturdy rubber hose. It could bent, stretched, or even traveled through. But history was just that, a past story, and a new action could not alter it. History found a way to repair itself. If Baxter had not died that night by the paws of the tiger, he would have surely been killed shortly thereafter, rectifying the fact that he had lived past the point when he was supposed to leave this dimension. It was remarkable that the professor looked so much like someone in his family.

Who's future would end? Were those guys the ones that had given him the TTC? If so, why then had they stopped him from killing the tiger? Then Jacob thought of her. Lily. That was how she had signed her name. Lily had all the answers. She was the one he needed to talk to. The person to see. He thought about the perfume on the letter. It reminded him of Grace…and why had Lily signed her name and ended it the same way that Grace had always done. Yes, Lily was the answer to mostly all of his questions. He must find her. She had said that she would be waiting. Jacob thought out loud, "Okay, future, I'm going to find you. Please be there."

Shadow came into the room and walked around on the clothes in the floor and jumped up on the bed and sat there staring up at him. Jacob looked back and reached down and scruffed the top of Shadow's head and then walked off rambling through the house to think of what he would do next.

Jacob stood in the shower with the water running over his face. He stared upward, eyes closed, feeling the almost too hot water run over his face and down his body. He stood there, lavishing the warmth, but shivered at the thought of finding out the truth. He was searching for the truth about everything, if there was such a thing.

Unknown to Jacob was that the transfer in Tut's tomb was part and parcel to neutralizing his action against Baxter? But what really happened was that Baxter was a step ahead and removed her from the stream of her very essence. Lily was just gone. The silk scarf still tied around her waist. Then there were the others, attempting good, which was also a part of this tug of war for her.

Chapter 18

"Cob. Hey man, sit down have a drink. Haven't seen you in a coon's age. What's going on with you?" Chandler asked.

"Man, I'm doing alright. Just waiting to hear about wha's happening with my work at this job and not much else. Coolin' out mainly. What about you? What ya been up to?" continued Cob.

"Not much. Just glad I didn't have to go over to Nam. Man, I've heard some weird shit about what went on over there. I heard you were over there with my brother." Chandler said.

The mood chilled. Smoke all around the dimly lit room and an odd scent that Cob recognized but couldn't give it any real credence. Otis Redding bellowed out from the jukebox at the end of the bar facing the door. Sitting on the Dock of the Bay. Cob got another chill just at that moment and tucked his chin down flat to his upper chest. Cob's mind was elsewhere as all the conversation just left, until, "Hey Man," Cob finally heard from the jukebox 'been loving you too long to stop now.

Chandler was almost yelling "Hey, Hey, Cob, you in there? I believe someone here either got put out or trying to get back home after some doing, Hey Man ya doing ok? Did I disturb you or anything?"

"Naw, Naw, man, come on its good to see you. What's been going on with you? You know, nobody sings that song like Aretha." Otis' Try a little Tenderness was playing now.

"Ya got that right," Chandler agreed.

"Tell me wha's been going on with you?" Cob queried.

"Oh, not much, I'm just working like a, should I say, a gov'ment mule."

"I heard that" Jacob remarked. "So what have you been doing other than having the other mules fartin' in your face?" They both laughed and avoided touching as they each reached for the boiled eggs in the black bowl in the middle of the table.

Cob looked around and realized that it had been a long time since he'd been there. Peanut shells littered the floor and the waitress came with another bowel of nuts and more eggs on the table.

"'Nother beer?"

"Yea, yea, give me another. You know, Chandler, I believed that after Grace, was gone, I'd never be involved with anyone again."

"Man, don't tell me you've met someone...?" His sentence left hanging just because he had more to ask, but thought he could find out more if he just left it open.

"Well, not exactly. It's just that I sometimes feel like I'm being stalked. This woman, I see her everywhere."

"Oh yeah? I bet it's one of your students—you remember how crazy 18, 19-year-olds can be."

Cob changed the subject with, "I see by the ring on your hand you got hitched up, when did this happen?"

"Yeah, man, got me a ball and chain"

"Naw it can't be that bad." Cob joked.

"Well, I'm just saying that, it's good man, it's good." He quickly changed the subject, too.

"So how long were you in Nam?"

"Too long." Cob answered. His mind's eye showed him the mud and tall grass of the jungle he's walked through carrying a weapon and other survival gear.

Chandler saw the weary sleepless nights on Jacob's face, the rungs under his eyes and the scruffy beard just coming through.

Chandler's words bounced around their table but never quite landed in Cob's ear until he heard, "You were there with Baxter weren't you?" he said a second time.

Cob took in a noisy breath as if he were about to gasp or had just heard bad news. His chocolate brown skin glistened in a gulf of sweat that beaded 'round about his forehead. He moved his clinched hands under the table to his thighs and clinched his teeth.

"Oh, man, Chandler, I was so sad about his death." The second Jacob heard Baxter's name he also heard rushing water like a river or waterfall. Cob turned his head toward the silent jukebox. There were no other sounds for that moment, just his own in sympathy to Chandler and himself. The sting of Baxter's death rang loud. Each man stared past the other, lost in memories; one wanted to keep forever, the other to erase completely.

"Last time I saw him," Chandler recalled, "was when we took him to the airport and waited for him to walk through the gate. Bax said, ' Man, I will see you in a year and I'll whip your ass on the court.' I told him, Baca, man you ain't quick enough to whip me with those big ol' feet. Remember to step high, so those dogs of yours don't get you into any trouble." He said it again, "you ain't quick enough to beat me..." it was almost a song the way Chandler said it as he lingered on the 'me' letting it dangle and then just drop. "Yep I told him that he couldn't even hold a ball and I know couldn't get to the hoop with me on him."

Chandler pulled his cap down a bit on his forehead and tightened his lips as if he were trying to keep words in. "Man, its hard to know," Chandler looked away sort of toward the skintight hotpants the waitress wore, without finding the sentence he wanted to complete.

Looking back at Cob, Chandler said, "They sent his things. Mama gave them to me, but the box is still in the closet." He searched for more words. "She opened it once, but kinda doesn't want anything to do with it anymore. I don't know why, he was her favorite, we all knew that." He dropped that, and let it hang for a moment. "We rarely talk about Baca unless someone sees a picture of him on the table and asks who it is? Mama just says 'That's my oldest boy, he run off to the Army and got hisself kilt in that Nam place, yes, Vietnam place. They didn't even send any little bit of him home neither, just his old stuff' Then she leaves the room and nobody says anything else about him. But you know, Cob? Sometimes I feel like he's right in the house with us…playing his dirty little tricks on us."

"Oh, you and your wife still live at your mom's house?" Cob asked.

"Naw, man, I bought a house down the street. One day after Daddy died, Momma was laying down on the couch and—now this is what she said,—'a little bird was tappin on me, and I could feel his breathing on my face, and when I opened my eyes, there was fire everywhere.' I grabbed my hat and I was so glad I left my wig in it when I lay down. Then I grabbed my pictures off the table of all my babies and my husband and me, my purse was on my arm and that little bird showed me where the door was. I wonder how that bird got in my house,' she said. I think she still looks for it, first thing she does when she goes outside is look up in the trees."

"You know, it could have been an angel that showed up in a form that wouldn't scare her" Cob replied, "God works in mysterious ways and…" Cob stopped when he saw Chandlers face change. A surprised shout—mostly air but Cob could hear it.

"God didn't have to take my brother! Did He?"

Cob placed his hand on Chandler's forearm.

"I ask that same question everyday about 'why, why,...is my wife gone?"

They both paused a minute from any conversation or acknowledgement that either were there.

"Y'all alright? 'Nother beer?" The waitress interrupted their thoughts.

"Sure," they said in unison, and then Chandler added, "make it two for each."

She left a bowl of popcorn this time. At first she turned to go but turned back and said, "Y'all want somethin' to eat? We got samwiches and chili." She handed them the menus that were printed on sandwich-size brown paper bags.

When the waitress came back with their beer she said, "Y'all really in a blow up conversation back here...I was scared to come over that one o' y'all send me out of here, drowning in yo river of sorrow. Ya ok?"

"Yea, yea, 'just talking about Vietnam."

"I know what you mean. A lot of guys used to come in here got lost over there—ain't coming back—some died, some just run off, they say and some just disappeared," she sighed. "It sho was a shame, wasn't it?" She didn't wait for an answer but picked up the bags with their orders marked and walked to the next table with a bubbly greeting.

Chandler and Cob glanced at each other and quickly channeled their gaze to the popcorn bowl knowing that they needed a minute or two before more words could be said.

"Can I ask you something? Now if you don't want to answer, I do understand," Cob said.

"What?"

"You said you feel Baxter is sometimes there playing tricks on you? What did you mean? I mean to say...do you see his image?"

"Why you ask me that, man?" Chandler growled.

Cob leaned back in the chair and kept his wrists on the table. He took a deep breath of the dusty, musty air, smelling of the people, the food cooking right behind them, and the beer he just drank on his own breath.

"Its just that I feel Grace, sometimes…its like she's trying to tell me something or giving me messages, ya know, warnings…" He left the sentence and looked around the room as he heard that wildlife sound of a rolling, rushing river. He looked around the room for water running.

"Hey, Cob, you looking for someone?"

"Naw, I just thought I heard something that usually…"

"That usually what?"

"Usually I just hear when I'm alone, you know, at home, in the quiet."

"In the night-time, huh?" Chandler asked, with his gritty little half smile under his unkempt moustache.

"No just during my alone time. At home, in any of the rooms—even in the back yard, but mostly…"

"Mostly where?"

Cob waved his hand down like he was getting ready to dribble a ball and closed it to make a fist and wrapped it with his other hand.

"Its silly."

"Naw man, ain't nothing about this stuff silly." Chandler said. "Its like I feel Baca coming out of the storage area where his things that came back from Nam are kept."

"Okay, okay, its just that she's in the kitchen. I smell food cooking and the cat, her cat, is fed, and I know I didn't do it. Is that what you meant by tricks he plays on you?"

"Wow!" Chandler looked both ways to see if anyone was listening to him. "Kinda. The house gets angry if we bring in certain types of food. First, Momma don't let us bring in no kind of Chinese or Asian food. She thinks it's all the same."

He continued, "Now don't laugh, this is for real."

"What' ja mean—certain kinds of food?" Cob threw right back at him.

"Like ribs or pork chops. Momma don't cook chitlins no more, and Daddy used to love him some pig feet and hog maws, even though nobody else in the house could stand them when we were all living at home as little kids. I brought a part of a ham sandwich home one day, and I swear that Baxter came up to me and without real words you could hear, told me to put it in the garbage, and even louder told me to take the garbage outside the house."

"What'ja do?"

"I took the shit outside and put it in the garbage, and ain't nobody brought any pork in the house since, not even hot dogs or ribs. Now you know I loved me some ribs, but its just eerie now."

Maybe it was like testing the waters when the food came. Both, unknown to the other, had ordered ham and cheese sandwiches.

They busted out laughing and talked about old times before war. They selectively recalled only the fun stuff. They laughed and slapped five when one outdid the other in who had the best story. Pool games were starting up in the back, the music was louder, the voices all around more intense, and so they left.

They gave their best, 'we are from the old school handshake' and promised to keep in touch, but neither, at the time, intended to. Cob almost air walked to his car after finally remembering where it was parked. He looked around but Chandler must have been long gone. Then he had to figure out which car was his.

"I ain't drinking like that any more." He said out loud. His voice surprised even him and he looked around to see if there was anyone else out there. He covered his mouth as if to hold in any more outbursts. He scratched his face and upper lip as he felt his nappy beard was poking through his skin. "Whew, what a night." There was nothing there, only the sound of running water, like a river.

The car door was easy to open once he found the right key. He sat there, touched the seat of the passenger side then laid his head on the steering wheel and said, "Who is in here?" There was no other sound but the river he had heard off and on throughout the evening.

His next conscience thought was taking off his shoes as he entered the back door of his house through the garage. Hurriedly he made his way to the bathroom, with all those sounds of water his only thought was that he had to pee. His pants just dropped to the floor and since his aim wasn't quite right, he stepped out of the pants on the wet floor and vowed to clean it up tomorrow. "Who are you? " he asked as he was lead to his bedroom and helped under the covers. He sunk into dreamless sleep as the covers draped over him completely.

Chapter 19

Ben sat at a small wooden desk in his garage, the kind a kindergartner teacher used, surrounded by equipment. The garage door was closed and the entry into the house was not visible.

There was a florescent light over the desk and Ben was typing on a word processor. He would type, wait a minute then type again. The last message he typed was, "Yes, he is home, all is quiet." A message came back: "Did we create an uncontrollable monster here?"

"I'll work with him. I'll take responsibility for what he gets into and keep you posted." Ben typed back.

There was no response to that. Ben reached up and pulled the top down to the machine that he kept under lock and key, hidden away from nosey neighbors and prankster kids. When closed, the top read TTC in subtle gold letters.

***

It had been almost a week since Jacob had returned from his travel back to the 1970's Vietnam and his aborted attempt to save his friend Baxter. He had been fading in and out of a sickening depression, thinking about the whole picture show he lived through again but now finally he felt he had some grasp on what had actually happened...that he truly was not responsible for Baxter's death. Jacob stood at the window, looking out at the evening before him. The night was crystal clear and he could see the lights on the harbor flickering in the clarity of the atmosphere. A cruise ship bobbed while being refitted for another cruise of the coast.

Now that I have it all together, he thought, he needed to tell someone to see how much sense it made. *It still doesn't make sense to me;* He went back over the events of the last couple of weeks in his mind, chronologically lining everything up as it happened. Jacob knew now that the feeling he had at Fisher's Point was the first real idea that something strange was happening and that his mind wasn't playing tricks on him. He went back to the same spot to find that feeling or have it repeated. Nothing.

He thought again about going back to find Grace but he could not face the pain of seeing her die again, drown again…not if he couldn't bring her back for real and forever and keep her safe.

The car, yes, the car, he had seen at the Point definitely had something to do with it. He had seen the car again when he arrived home and then…the package. Jacob thought about the contents of the package. It was all real, he hadn't thought so at first but he knew now that it was all real. There was a woman somewhere who he had to contact so that she could help him put all of this together and he could make some kind of sense of it.

Oh, yes, the book, he thought. Suddenly his book came to mind because it was about the places he had gone and things he had seen. He was so tempted to read it…suddenly Jacob noticed movement out of the corner of his eye as he stood just outside the door. He could see the top of his neighbor's head as he turned back toward his house. Ben had been looking over the fence. Jacob thought that Ben would be a good person to bounce all of this off, to see if Ben was or could be a believer. Jacob went back into the house to get the TTC and the book.

He rustled through the desk drawer and removed the letter Lily and the one from Grace for comparison. He stood there looking at the objects trying to decide if there was anything else he wanted to bring, what was he missing? Jacob walked out through his garage and headed for Ben's front door when he saw there was light inside the garage. Rather than knock, he walked to the side of the house and found the side entrance to the garage door ajar. He started to call out but could hear Ben working somewhere behind the many scattered crates and boxes. Jacob walked around a box and saw Ben working at his desk with his back to him. He was engrossed in typing.

Jacob called. "Hey, Ben, what you doing?"

Ben quickly turned to see Jacob standing there behind him. He closed the top of what appeared to be a computer game board and quickly put it in the desk drawer. "Hey Jacob, howya doin? I didn't hear you come in."

"I didn't interrupt anything, did I?" Jacob asked.

"No, not at all. I was just finishing up a report for some associates."

Jacob stared at the drawer where Ben had placed the contraption; something seemed familiar about it, which returned his focus to why he was there.

"Jacob what you got there?" Ben asked. Jacob handed the TTC to Ben. Ben took it, looked it up and down, turned it over and then opened it. "Nice game case."

Jacob shook his head, "it's not a game case; it is a machine. Now, don't think I've lost all my marbles, but it's a *TIME* machine.

"Yeah, right!" Ben said. "and your name is HG Wells, you know!" Jacob just looked at Ben, his shoulders drooping as far down as he could get them, feeling somewhat silly.

"I am doing this all wrong." Jacob said. "Here, read this." He handed Ben the letter from Lily. Ben took the letter, handed the TTC back to Jacob and began to read. The look on his face said, "Are you kidding me?" but he said nothing, but paced across the garage floor. Jacob stood there waiting as Ben continued reading.

"Well?" Jacob said.

Ben looked back at him and sort of muttered, "Is there more: I mean there must be more to it than this!"

Jacob said, "Okay, sit down and let's see if I can bring you up to snuff on what has been happening. About two weeks ago, I was really in the greatest pit of the dumps in terms of how my life was and still is now and feeling really bad and I'm missing Grace so much." He paused. "I went down to The Point to think and that is when I got this feeling that someone was watching me." Jacob went on chronologically laying out the events of the last couple weeks.

When he finished talking, Jacob felt the coolness of sweat on the back of his neck. The perspiration was running down the middle of his back. It felt as if he just re-lived the entire ordeal for the third, fourth or fifth time. He'd stopped counting. The coolness of the garage now gave him a chill. He had just relived the horror of it all. As much as Jacob wanted to rid himself of this feeling, it still lingered. They sat there staring at each other. The silence between them was ominous, penetrating the very room itself until Ben finally said, "Jacob, do you really believe what you just told me?" Jacob stared back in disbelief.

"Look Jacob, you have been going through a lot of stress recently with the death of your wife and all. Hell, man, I would be going crazy, too, if I had gone through that kind of thing. Mind you I'm not saying you are crazy or anything like that, it's just that...well, at times like these, we sometimes mix dreams with reality and...Well, it just all gets confused. Do you understand what I am trying to say, son?"

Jacob thought, *No he didn't understand. Is Ben telling me that he did not believe any of this? That can't be, all the evidence is here, the book, the letter and most of all, the TTC.* "I am not going crazy, Ben, and this is not a fantasy," Jacob finally said. "I brought this to you hoping that you could give me some insight as to what this all means."

"Okay, you want my opinion? Let it go. Drop this nonsense about time travel and futuristic women and such."

Jacob held the book up. "How do you explain this?"

"Just like you told me, an elaborate hoax probably designed by one of your students," Ben countered. "Maybe that Tommy or Tony kid who wrote that paper you told me about, that was a bit out there, ya know. Maybe you dreamed all this after you graded that paper.

This was a mistake. Jacob thought *I should never have come here. Now Ben thinks I am some kind of nut.*

He picked up the letter and the TTC, "You know, you're probably right about all of this. I'm sorry I bothered you. It was kind of just going around in my head. Like you said, I have probably just been under too much stress. Hey, thanks for your time, man. I gotta go."

Ben eyed him suspiciously, "What are you going to do?"

"I think I will take a little vacation, go somewhere and get some rest." "That sounds like a good idea. What do you say we get together, say,

Saturday? We can talk about it some more. Maybe I can help you figure out some place for you to go and get that rest. I know some pretty good spots that are remote and restful. I own a small cabin in the Cascade Mountains with a friend of mine. If you want my advice, go for fun and rest in between."

Ben followed Jacob out of the garage. The night air chilled Jacob to his bones. He turned and Ben shook his hand, he then walked back toward his house.

"Hi ya, Jacob?" said Cora, "Oh, you found Ben in there? I tell you, that man just disappears sometimes." Just then Jacob felt a bit of a chill again.

"Have you been okay? I mean, I don't see much of you anymore. It must be very difficult for you right now. The pain will go away in time...but the sorrow never really does. Grace will always live in your heart and that's what you've got to hold on to. Now to change the subject, why don't you accept any of our dinner invitations? I'm not a great cook, but the food will fill you and the conversation could be a plus. Might be a little better than having meals with that cat of yours. Look at me hogging the conversation. How are you? "

Jacob forced a small grin; "I'm doin okay, Cora, how about you and Little Bit over there? She is really growing up and cute as she can be."

"You know, I just baked a batch of cookies and made way too many. I know you like oatmeal pecan, so you wait right here and I'll get some for you."

"Great. You better believe I will wait for cookies. Hey little Cora," Jacob said as Hannah entered the room from the hallway. "What have you been doing fun this week?"

"Not much but I'm going to see the real Mickey Mouse and the Mousekateers."

"Oh yeah? When are you going to do that?"

"In a few minutes. But then we'll be right back in a few minutes after that so you won't even miss us and we won't skip any minutes, either."

Cora burst in, handed over the plastic bag filled with warm cookies and quickly escaped through the kitchen doors with Hannah in tow. "See you later Jacob," Cora said. " I've got to get her ready for tomorrow. Enjoy the cookies." She waved and hurried Hannah into the other room.

As Jacob entered his front door, Shadow trotted over and rubbed up against his shoe. He walked down to the den and placed the TTC, book and letter on the table. Yes, he knew exactly where he was going to go. *Okay, Lily, you asked me to come to where you are…and here I come. I hope you are still there and not just a figment of my imagination.*

He counted up all the facts he knew about Lily. *Oh this is ridiculous,* he thought. She was daring, kinda cute, He had seen that much of her in the car when she was here. He looked into the bathroom mirror trying to figure out what she wanted from him, why she had chosen him, and what this was all about, a crusade with the past? He showered and shaved and patted his face with his favorite cologne. Then he grabbed the wet face towel and wiped his face clean of cologne. He did not want to…to what? *Hell, this isn't a date, and I need answers,* he thought. There were too many whys, and Lily held all the answers.

The one person that Jacob thought would understand and believe all of this had surprised him. In fact, Ben had been rather nonchalant about the whole thing.

Jacob's mind spun. He was missing something. Shadow followed him from room to room as Jacob tried to process that last confounding thought. *No, it couldn't be.*

Jacob retrieved a half-gallon carton of milk from the fridge and poured some into Shadow's bowl then drank some from the carton himself. He wanted something cold, anything, even milk.

Shadow rubbed up against Jacob's shoe to say 'thank you' then slurped up the milk. Jacob went into the den still holding the milk carton. *What was it that Ben said or was it something he had done…that was bothering him.* He continued to wrestle with this thought as he continued to drink the iced cold milk from he carton.

Jacob picked up the letter from Lily. She checked the coordinates for her location which, according to this, would be somewhere near Seattle, Washington. Well, he was ready. It was time to solve some of this mystery and he could see no reason to delay it any longer. Jacob reached for the TTC and as he did, the bracelet he had worn for Baxter slid down his wrist. He turned it so he could read the name and date. *Has it been that long?*

Time passed and he changed, almost everything else changed, too. Now he was going to clear up some other events. He wanted to know why all these things that occurred in his life were happening. He took the bracelet off.

Jacob thought long and hard about the conversation he'd had with Chandler. There was still something really missing in all this. Jacob looked at Shadow and said, "Have I lost my complete mind?" Shadow just turned his head to the side like he really understood what was being said and trotted off.

Right out loud he shouted, "Yes, I have lost my whole damn mind talking with the crazy ass dwarf cat. What the hell is happening to me?" He stared at the picture of himself and his wife on the mantle taken the day they married. He looked at it as if to study everything there and said to the photo, "If you want to come back and even play dirty tricks on me its, ok." He said it louder…"ITS OK!" Then held his head in his hand as if his neck could no longer do that. *There is something I've got to do. But what is it?*

Grace had always said, "the universe will tell you what it needs from you."

Yeah right. It ain't talking lately. He still found little notes Grace had left for herself all over the house. She even addressed them to herself, some of the notes read, Dear Grace, listen, to your spirit. Dear Grace, All you need to realize your every dream is inside you. He found the messages taped to the cabinet doors in the medicine cabinet and on closet walls. The last one he found stopped him cold. Dear Grace, hold on to your passion for life, it is forever in you to hold on to all you love. Stepping away from one life does not mean you step away from the love it holds. He had torn it off the wall and held it to his chest until the tears were gone. He taped it to a bigger piece of paper and placed it with all the other items that he remembered were precious to her. Embracing her belongings...her favorite shawl, and her last knitting project, he looked out the window toward the sky, "Grace, you can hold onto me." He announced in a whisper.

Chapter 20

Jacob did not go back to look for Lily. Something just held him back. Each time he got ready, rehearsed his questions and practiced his stance, he chickened out. *She could be a Jezebel or worse.* He tucked that thought away whenever it reared its ugly head.

However, Jacob traveled back to the battlefield in Vietnam on many occasions, each time observing and realizing something new, creating his own de je vue. Sometimes what he found there were extra people; they were present and he didn't know how he could have missed them before. He didn't recognize the faces of any of the other time travelers.

At one of Jacob's visits there was a woman…but no women were ever in direct combat in 1969—70; what's *a nurse doing here*? He thought. He heard the troupe coming, *there comes the guys…no only one, me! Wow, that's me. That's right, I was the lead man.* He thought, he noticed the tiger on the other side of the clearing and a pig. The woman appeared suddenly and threw something in the middle of the clearing and out sprang the tiger as a pig went to what he thought was his dinner. Instead, he became the tiger's appetizer.

*Why couldn't there be a whole bunch of those damn pigs? That would give all the guys a chance to live and…*He looked away as the jaws of the tiger clamped the back of the unsuspecting swine. The squeal, barely audible as its spirit left the body of the kitty's evening snack. When his eyes retuned to the scene, tiger was walking toward the bushes, swinging the pig. The pig's body gave a quick jerk from one of its legs then they just dangled limply.

He turned to see where the men were at that point, and the nurse stood right in front of him. "Don't do anything else stupid," she said to him. "I can always find you. Remember that." She disappeared.

I know that face, he thought. *Where have I seen her?*

Sometimes he felt that life was crashing in on him with so many people in and out of his life only, seconds at a time. He used to think these visits were just his imagination or dreams. Now he knew they were real. He exited as the men entered the clearing and found the blood.

***

Professor Stevens was a nervous wreck as he tried to figure out what happened to Kaye. Her realm age should have been less than 35 years old, however, her physical body age was nearing at least a century.

He continued to search for the diaries and based on the diaries, Lily shared with him and Lily's ability to translate the documents and other writings; he felt he was about to locate Kaye at a place where the others could not reach her.

Stevens needed to find the precise second in time and space before her capture in order to get her back the way she was, her 'normal' self.

Program after program, after program he examined and nothing, but he knew he was close.

Stevens decided he had to talk to Ben in a face-to-face session to find out what had been done. When the professor arrived Ben and Cora were relaxing outside, bare feet nestled comfortably in the newly manicured lawn. There was a pleasant feeling in the air as if a kind spirit of sorts was also there. Just then Hannah, came bounding through with her drink hanging from a lanyard around her neck. The straw just barely tickled her chin as she merrily passed through the middle of the adults' conversation singing a funny little song that captured children at an amusement park. Her humming and gobbledygook words made no sense at all until she ended with "Is a small world after all."

"Damn" he shouted suddenly? "It's not far from me—it's in my own circle."

"What's in your circle, Stevens?" asked Ben.

"I think I know where..." he stopped.

"I'll see you in a while." He was gone.

Ben and Cora went back to their conversation and it was as if Hannah had said nothing. The bird on her shoulder began to repeat, "I'm ok, I'm ok."

He found Kaye tucked away not too far but very obscured from any of them. He took her home and nursed her back to health but could not reverse her transition.

"Kaye you know a lot has happened during your absence. And I have to find out how I can reverse the script you were to follow to oblivion."

A resounding sigh escaped from Kaye. "If I return to normal then Lily will be lost going backwards. You know they tried to take us both and use all our time when they couldn't they just split it so the older I become, the younger Lily is and she loses her time. But when I reverse she too will return to childhood."

"Okay," he said. "While you are here, let's work on you. Okay?"

"Sure." Kaye was exhausted.

"Now explain to me what happened, here at this juncture."

"Have Lily show you her computations. Do you know were she is?"

"Yes, she's safe. You're safe here, too, so I'll go now." And he did.

Lily was able to decipher the formulas to the 32nd degree.

It worked! Kaye was again restored to her proper age and in her right mind. But Lily could not be found and no one could even imagine her condition. *A paradox did exist, but what?* Stevens thought.

***

Jacob was about to meet Lily and truly remember her, but he was snatched away by PawPaw. Kaye realized that something was terribly wrong and went to rescue Lily and she missed by one beat then realized they were together. Ben and Cora were there as back up and Hannah was just there. Watching.

Other entities were there as well. Baxter wanted more time and didn't care where it came from. He saw what he felt were 'easy pickins.' Chandler kept his distance and Tony was hovering. They all missed their mark, this time.

Everything was back to normal with the exception of Lily. The universe knew, and everything else was just wishful thinking.

Chapter 21

After Stevens located Kaye, she worked night and day to make sure she left no stones unturned in her search for Lily. The experiment Lily and Kaye attempted was to see how they could go back in age as well as time. In their thwarted attempt to get away from their captives, they were at the mercy of evil. They'd still agreed that only one would go back at a time and the other would make sure she got back to her own realm.

Lily was supposed to go back only to ten years. Somewhere there had been interference. But where? Evidently the mark was missed because Lily didn't show up at the top of the stairs one foot from the attic door, when she should have. They should have only been seconds apart but somehow all was askew. Kaye didn't know about the side trip Lily took to meet Jacob in Egypt at first. The Tut rendezvous was interrupted with Jacob and Kaye wasn't aware of any of that. She just knew that whatever time Lily had fallen into, was detrimental to her friend, and she, too, was in danger.

Maybe Lily was thrown to a different path if the atmospheric pressure was different or a storm passed through her stream. *What did we miss?* Thought Kaye. They had gone to their childhood years together before and it all appeared safe and secure. Kaye realized there must have been interference from an outside element and it had been there all along. Just waiting for an opportunity.

This other element must be a spirit that has an unclear but unscrupulous intent. There was no real evidence…but was there, somewhere. *No he's there.* Kaye realized she was indeed looking for a person, a male person. But who? Something had changed, but what? There were differences that she could see and feel. Things like dwindling food supply; there was contaminated water, strange diseases and other world catastrophes.

She went back to that time when and where Lily was to meet her and found that something strange about the people she discovered there. Kaye believed that you must correct things if you see something wrong, out of place, changed or purposely deadly. So finding a moving, roving individual was harder than finding a needle in a haystack. Kaye didn't quite know where to start. It was as if she were combing the air, someone could be right behind her or even more frightening, just ahead, and she wouldn't be the wiser.

She remembered someone told her once that in all things she had to know who her enemies are and where they are. This same someone also told her to be careful of smiling faces and those who appeared to have no reason to offer her a smile, especially when the eyes don't match it.

Kaye knew she'd been in the right area though, because Lily left one unseasonable candy cane lying conspicuously in the vegetable bin. *She's been here!* Kaye thought. Her whole being puffed up wanting to scream a happy laugh just knowing that she was in the vicinity of her friend. Maybe.

***

Jacob realized he'd collided with someone or something, not knowing what happened he just stuck the candy cane in his jacket lapel. Kaye continually visited lots of times in different hours searching for more clues.

***

In that exact instant, on a different dimension, "This child has been here before. Just look at her, that's an old soul." Lily, in the corner, played nonchalantly with her doll, Lily Grace. She hung onto every word spoken to find out what was going to happen to her.

Kaye learned that Lily was in the 20th century because she had gone too far back in her own age and inadvertently, centuries. Three centuries, to be exact. Well, she had set up enough clues for herself to find Lily but something was off. *Something was not in its rightful place. This was even more difficult than finding that good-for-nothing needle in a haystack. More like a certain individual grain of sand dropped in the middle of the ocean—find that.* She thought.

Kaye also knew that there was a devious spirit following her. *The devious spirit just has to be Jacob's,* she thought. *It has to be.* He wanted to stop her from stopping him, but she wasn't sure that he knew she saved his life from the tiger, setting the pig in his place. The tiger was meant for Baxter for a reason. She now wished she'd not made that change because she believed he was pursuing her in a death rage. So she'd been lured to Jacob's original time. Kaye thought that was where Lily was stuck.

All equipment and identifiers were confiscated so now Lily was lost, even from Baxter. After dozens of transfers to different families and homes Lily had been left to grow up in a home up the street from the park. They called her Grace because someone made the comment when she was found most definitely abandoned, this is truly God's Grace that this child survived. Lily had no idea how she got to where she was or who she was. Everything was foreign to her. But, it was as if she knew of this place, but barely.

Kaye remained in the 20th century searching, returning to her own time daily to just see if Lily returned, which she hadn't. Kaye kept up appearances in the visited time to give validity to her existence saying that her late husband left her well-suited. Since professions enamored most of the folks in this era, Kaye identified herself as a writer. When asked about her writing, she'd pull hundred-year-old books from her own time and mask them as her own creation. Who would know? She kept her name so that her own time mates could find her if something happened.

"Do you mind if I sit here? There just aren't any more seats and I tell you, my feet are killing me. I can't figure that out either, this never happens to me, I can walk for hours, usually."

Kaye looked up from her newspaper and saw a big eyed, young, beautiful, dark skinned woman with big hair and shiny lip-color and loud blue color on her eyelids. . "Oh no, go right ahead." As she looked away, a tiny flicker of light flashed at the corner of her right eye. At that moment Kaye knew that she had to pay attention to everything and everyone especially this woman. The last time that happened she discovered time travel, so therefore a message, a clue, a sign was there; someplace close.

"Were you waiting for someone?" the woman asked Kaye.

"No, just trying to get caught up on the news of the day." Kaye went back to reading the paper, the personals, really because she'd put an ad in saying she was looking for her cat. The ad offered a $50 reward for the cat's return.

"I see you are going through the ads. Anything in there interesting?" motor mouth continued.

Kaye stopped, folded the paper and waited for the chatty woman to say something that gave her any reason to listen.

"I come here every day, and I've never seen you here before. Are you from around here or did you just move to the neighborhood?"

"Brand new to the neighborhood," Kaye remarked. She was looking for something, a sign or clue to where she could find Lily, so she just tightened her teeth together and sucked in air through them.

"Where about?" said the woman.

"Not too far, but tell me about the area. It looks really like there are just wonderful folks and plenty of little shops."

"Oh yes, the grocery store is brand new and you don't have to catch a bus to get there from here. The manager will even let you take the cart home with your groceries, if you bring it right back like within a couple of hours."

"Do they have a lot of really good fresh fruit and vegetables?" asked Kaye.

"Oh yes, the produce is fresh everyday. Or," the woman leaned over closer as if to tell a secret, "To save a few pennies, you can move into the midsection and pick up one of the day old leftovers." Without taking a breath she continued, "I sometimes get that when it's a real good deal, or when I get it home I blanch it so that I can cook it fully within the week. My freezer isn't too big so I sometimes just cook it and put the stuff in canning jars and put hot wax over it and I know it will keep 'til my husband wants that certain vegetable, and then he's surprised that I could have it all prepared that quick." She finally took a breath.

"Do you have children?"

"Oh, yes four boys, they are so rambunctious, makes me tired just thinking about it, now since the schools are so overcrowded that they have half day sessions I made sure that they all went in the morning together, you know, so that they could protect each other. The lady down the street keeps these State kids, you know the ones whose parents are doing who knows what and don't take care of them you know what I mean, don't you?" Not waiting for an answer, "I made sure mine go to school together so that they can protect each other," she repeated.

"Protect each other from what," Kaye asked wondering why she was even entertaining the crazy lady with any conversation.

"Why other kids, you know, some aren't brought up right and where I grew up we didn't go to school with no white kids and it was better 'cause we knew all the parents and we could talk to them if they had problems which could cause my kids any problems, but its different up here."

"Where did you originally come from then?" Kaye was now trying to get as much information as she could because there was a tone of something coming up that she needed to know.

"Oh, I'm from Mississippi, Rollin Fork, Mississippi, we were dirt poor but had a lot of love for each other especially family. But the work was so hard and when my Jimmy Joe went to the Service, you know, the Army, he came back and said 'We ain't staying here no more.' I guess he got a taste of the world while he was gone so we all got in that old car of his and got a place to stay and I just had the two kids then and he got a good job, cause he had training, you see, from the Service, ya know, at the railroad, fixing things, you know it pays good. I worked for a while, ya know, while we was starting out fresh, I did day work, and it wasn't too bad just the hours I was away from my own place, Joe, that's my husband, you got a husband?" again, she didn't wait for an answer. " He wants people to just call him Joe now so that's what we do."

Kaye stood up and prepared to leave when the woman said "I should walk back up to that store, you know, I have to talk to the manager; somebody keeps putting candy in my string bean bag. I think its one of them cashiers, they do dumb stuff like that you know."

"What?"

"Oh, those cashiers do all kinds of silly stuff."

"No, no, before that"

"Oh, about my string beans? I told you they have really nice vegetables and other produce."

"Yes, the sting beans, that's so interesting, what do they put with your string beans?"

"Oh, those Christmas candy things, uh, uh, candy canes. yeah, that's them."

Kaye took the woman by the hand and said, "Please walk me to that store. I need to see all those great bargains you've been telling me about. They should make you the Welcome Wagon Hostess of the whole area you have such wonderful information."

The lady looked a bit puzzled, staring at Kaye over the top of her glasses her eyebrows almost touching. "Well, I wanted to finish my coffee, it's getting a little cold now. Come on, let's go. You are really gonna love shopping in here."

She continued chattering as they walked and Kaye, kept stopping her from wandering into the many little shops on the way.

Just as they got to the grocery store, the woman said. "Well, I have to go now cause my boys will be home soon."

"Yes, I understand. You have been so helpful, just run along now." Kaye said and walked into the store.

Kaye nodded to different people she'd seen around the area, then found the grocer and asked where she could find string beans.

"Let me walk you over there," he said. "This is your first time here, isn't it?"

She nodded 'yes' and smiled excited beyond measure. He led her to the beans, and then disappeared to help another customer. Sure enough, as tears came to her eyes, there were several candy canes underneath, so this was no accident. Tears ran down her face. As she passed the candy boxes Kaye stuffed three string beans on the left side of the candy canes. Kaye knew she was ever so close to finding her friend.

Kaye haunted coffee shops and looked through old bookstores and museums with fourteenth century poets and chamber music and cello shops. She felt that she was close to finding her. She scanned over twenty years in the mid to late twentieth century, however, only thirty of her own days searching every inch of the City for Lily. *She's nowhere to be found.* Kaye thought. A concrete bench at the edge of the park's walkway invited her to rest. She accepted the invitation and laid her groceries next to her.

A bird chirped from some pine trees, just beyond her sight, and she leaned forward in her seat to get a look at the tiny creature, then saw that it was tropical and definitely out of place.

She whistled and it moved to a closer branch in response. It was gray and white, with bright yellow and orange feathers mixed in. She whistled again and it echoed her call. They stared at each other whistling every once in a while as if to just check in. Kaye leaned back a little to take in the clarity of the sky and the perfect, natural warmth of the sunshine on her skin. In her real time, air, temperature and sunshine were manufactured and controlled. She marveled at the perfect place God had given her just for this moment of perfect peace, to wash her mind of loss and doubt. She stood to stretch the tangles from her mind and body and raised her hands to the sky, to God, as if to say, "I give up." The bird landed on her wrist and said, "Hello." Startled, Kaye looked at the creature in disbelief and said, what did you say?" Knowing that it wouldn't repeat itself.

Bird answered, "I'm okay, I'm okay, hello, hello, hello." Kaye stepped back, placing her right hand over her heart and smiled. "Thank you God." The bird echoed, "thank you God, thank you God."

Four times that week Kaye came back to that park and the bird yelled out "hello, hello, hello."

"Hello bird." Kaye would answer, and raise her arm so the bird could perch there. The bird leaned his head down and allowed Kaye to rub his feathered crown, sometimes he even purred. Bird moved from her wrist, then arm, then shoulder, then chest. He'd sit there and stare at her face while she watched the sky and the trees and the people. Sometimes he'd ask "Are you in there?" And she'd respond with, "hello, hello, hello."

One-day bird laid his head on her chin, just under the curve of her lip. As she leaned her head down to accommodate the bird she looked down to see company. For a moment Kaye's intent was to protect the bird by placing her hand near his back, but the cat didn't seem interested in coming closer.

Just then she heard a familiar voice say "Shadow, are you bothering this lady? Stop that." Kaye's whirled around but careened herself so neither the cat nor this woman would be startled. Her eyes filled quickly with the tears of three centuries and the familiar voice said, "are you alright? Can I get you something? Can I call someone for you?"

"Oh no, thank you very much but I guess I was daydreaming I looked up right into the sun and the light got in my eyes."

"I'm okay, thank you."

The bird said, "I'm okay, I'm 'K, hello, hello, hello." Kaye grabbed the sunglasses from her pocket and quickly covered her eyes. It was Lily, a younger Lily.

"I must have startled you," said Grace. "I'm truly sorry. I believed that Shadow was pestering you for treats. I don't know how this cat gets out and finds his way over here at least two or three times a week; usually he gets here earlier in the day. Ya sure you're okay?"

"Oh, yes, I'm fine, thank you." Kaye made a funnel over her mouth and told Lily in a whisper, "If I say I'm okay that sets the bird off."

"That is such a cute bird, did you teach him to talk? "How long have you had him? A cockatiel isn't it?" Grace's questions actually ran right together, but Kaye was too full of joy to answer any of them. She knew she couldn't say anything that would make Grace afraid or uncomfortable with her. What would she do if someone she didn't remember ever meeting before just blurted out, "By the way, you are actually from the future and I've been looking for you for 200 years?"

"Yes, it is a cockatiel, and no, I didn't teach him to talk, he just started talking to me one day when I stopped here to rest. We've become friends. I'm sure he belongs to someone."

Grace pointed up the street. There's an open-air café over there you could put up a note to alert the owner and get some iced tea or something else cold to drink. They have covered tables too, so you can sit in the shade. Are you sure you're okay? My name is Grace, what about you?"

I'm Kaye and bird said, "I'm k, I'm 'k, I'm k, hello, hello, hello."

Kaye looked to the heavens and said out loud "thank you." Realizing what had just happened.

Grace gave her that raised eyebrow look. Kaye responded, "God answers prayer and just today I've received a blessing of knowledge I've been searching out for longer than you could ever imagine. Bird stayed perched on Kaye's shoulder and nibbled on her earring, while Shadow pranced along side Grace taking puppy steps as they walked along to the cafe.

They sat and talked for hours. Kaye asked questions about what she did and told her that she was new in the area. Grace told her she worked on lots of projects so she'd not be tied to any one thing but rather could fulfill lots of challenges and aspirations by completing one task at a time, devoting herself to that one only, then going on to something else. Kaye noticed a wedding ring and asked her about her family.

Grace said she was adopted and simply could not find out anything about her biological family so she stopped trying and yes, she was married. "To a wonderful man named Jacob, who teaches at the university only a block away from where we are sitting. In fact, we only moved to this neighborhood about a month ago, so we're still getting settled, too".

Kaye now visited the park often and knew she had to find a place nearby to live so that Grace could socialize with her. In walking distance of the park where she found Bird, Kaye established a living space for Grace's benefit. She even set up a place for Bird. She created a nameplate but made a typo, which she didn't notice until after it had been tacked and glued in place. The nameplate said "Brid," so that's what she called him.

Kaye brought many of Grace's belongings from her original time to her apartment, and each new item Grace would examine thoroughly and exclaim what interesting things Kaye owned; "ooooh, I wish I could find such nice things as these." And Kaye would retort, "Okay, that old thing, you can have it." Kaye tried very hard not to show excitement about getting closer to revealing many truths. Once she had to explain away a patent pending date, when Grace said, "this company's quality control unit missed this one—the date says April 22, 2147, that's weird."

"That's probably why it didn't cost much, you know, people make mistakes." Kaye added.

From then on Kaye always checked and removed dates on everything until she could figure out an appropriate manner to return Grace to her rightful time and regain her memory as Lily.

One day, while sitting in Grace's back yard, Jacob came home early and said, "Oh, now I get to meet the infamous Kaye. How do you do, Maam?"

Kaye was glad she'd worn a wide brimmed hat to keep the direct sun off her face. She avoided his eyes and exchanged niceties, finished her drink and turned the conversation to Grace, telling her she had to get ready for an old friend for dinner. Of course Grace wanted all the details.

"Oh, he's just a friend I've not seen for ages and ages so we are just going to remember old times."

"Sure, sure, Miss Kaye," said Grace, "I'll just ask Brid to tell me all, I mean everything, the next time I come over you know he will tell all he sees and hears."

As Kaye prepared to leave, first putting shoes back on her feet, the tender feel of the earth and grass on her soles made her feet want to break into a dance.

She just sat there kneading the ground, heel, toe, heel, and toe and absorbing all she could. As if the earth had special properties for any healing. "Oh, I see your neighbors are moving. Do you have new ones moving in soon?"

"Several couples have been looking, but I don't know yet who's bought the place," said Grace.

"I've met the man," said Jacob "he's a retired technology kind of guy. He seemed alright—on the almost stuffed shirt side of the dinning table, if you know what I mean—but very nice," Jacob remarked. "His name is Ben, that's all I remember."

"Do they have children?" Grace asked.

"Yes, a little girl. I guess the old dog's furnace is still lit," Jacob peered over the fence.

"The other couple sure left fast. I had no idea they were even thinking about moving." Said Grace. They said they got a really good offer from a company that was moving a semi retiree who felt this location was the best to study the sky or something like that." Grace said.

"Well," said Jacob, "he better keep his telescope pointed to his side of the sky." They all laughed.

Kaye, feeling very uneasy, headed for the door. Jacob was awaiting her with an outstretched hand, saying, "Please come back again real soon, and if you like, bring your friend, too."

"I certainly will. This has been a lovely afternoon. Thank you, Grace, for your charming hospitality."

"Don't forget, Kaye, we're going shopping next week."

"I'm looking forward to it."

After Kaye left and they all waved goodbye, Grace took the dishes from the patio to the kitchen and started the water in the sink to wash them when Jacob remarked, "She's an odd duck."

"Oh, stop."

"I mean don't you think she's kind of strange? It's like she's casing the joint."

"Yeah, yeah, sure. So you think she's gonna take something? We don't have anything here that we purchased new. No jewels, gold, silver, money or expensive anything, anyway. In fact she's given me many things from her apartment," Grace said. "Now what do we have of value here?"

Jacob gave her a look and said, "You, my darling, are the only object of priceless value here, and you are forever cherished. I'm crazy and I know it, but I hate to share the time I wanted to spend it with you, and I don't want to share you with anyone else, not even with that old crone."

She tightened her lips to hold back the outright laugh when he burst out laughing just looking at her trying not to. He grabbed her around the waist, kissed her on the top of her head, then on the forehead and said, "Hey, let's turn in early and go make a baby. Let's make ten babies."

She looked up, waiting for her real kiss and tighter hug, and said "Okay, give me a few minutes to straighten up the kitchen and take a quick shower, and

I'll be right there, before the news goes off, okay?"

"Okay."

Grace sang and danced through her kitchen ritual then showered and perfumed, but upon entering their bedroom she found Jacob sound asleep.

"Well, he's gone for the night." She went back to the den and started reading one of the books Kaye loaned her. The books were kind of futuristic and she found them fascinating. Kaye told her about old movies she liked from the 1940s and 50s—one in particular was, "Portrait of Jenny". Grace said she'd watch for it on late night old movies. Kaye researched the present time and learned that movie rental was very prominent, so she searched the shops to find movies that would introduce her friend to the concept without actually saying the words "time travel." She said it once and witnessed Grace cringe with uneasiness. Kaye had to be very careful to make sure that Grace was curious before she sprung any of the…real truth about who she was. She would have to be ready to leave this entire life behind.

Still, Kaye felt wickedness all around her as if something evil lurked near. Kaye had to carefully plan her next steps. Perhaps going back in this time to when Grace first remembers being and taking her back to the time she should be, she would think it out and make a plan with Stevens. However, there was definitely something else that needed to play out. *Who was trying to reach me or block me? She thought*

Fear brought a shudder through Kaye's whole being as she walked home. She had to make sure Jacob never wrote down her address. She'd move again next week. She walked into her apartment, opened Brid's cage, feed him and programmed the TTC to go home. She'd talk this over with Stevens. Ben would be there to keep an eye on Jacob, and perhaps provide some influence on his behavior.

Chapter 22

Professor Stevens sat at the table in Kaye's dining room, trying to orchestrate a plan to get Lily back to her rightful place and mind. To startle her would create even more havoc and she would not find her real self-intact. They decided to reveal small truths inch by inch until she "discovered" the real truth of who she was, where she was from and the dynamics of all the players.

Kaye and Professor knew now that they had to find the exact moment of Lily's transformation and go back minutes prior to avoid a further catastrophe created initially, they suspected, by Jacob. The problem was, only Jacob knew what had happened and, no one had access to the information of what had already happened, because Professor Stevens erased Jacob's memory of that time and of time travel in an effort to protect Kaye. He did this to prevent Jacob from changing things the way he said he would. Since he was a product of the 60s, Jacob wanted those he felt could save the world to live and prevent their untimely deaths.

Kaye and Stevens had to find the spirit that inhabited Jacob at the time of Kaye and Lily's transformation. Jacob was a bit wild and neither Kaye nor Stevens was sure of what he'd actually seen, done or learned during that short window of exploration through time during his then teen and early adult years.

"How can we unlock that knowledge without awakening the evil that created this turmoil in the first place?

"Can you find out if Grace is interested in the occult?"

"Why?"

"When the twentieth century folks run into something that they can't figure out, they believe it's an occult thing rather than examining it fully to find the true answer."

"They also believe that either God made it happen, if its good or the devil made them do something if the result is bad."

"So what are we? Good or bad?"

"That has no significance here, Stevens," snapped Kaye. "I just want my friend back and we both played a part in unleashing this chaos."

"Yeah, I know, how's Lily's oh, I mean Grace's memory when she sees and touches her belongings?"

"I think she's remembering something I've watched her staring into space with a blank expression, not a knowing stare but rather a questioning one."

"We could tell her I'm a hypnotist—"

"NO! Jacob would go berserk, and it might bring about an awakening in him that we don't want."

"What if we just take her back and..."

"No, she'd come back here to Jacob and we could lose her forever because she could die here, or then we could have two monsters." Kaye continued. "Grace has to be ready, she has to realize completeness and closure with this Jacob...only then will she go because she wants to, not just because we want her to, or she just unquestionably believes us."

"What kind of time line have you worked out for this, Kaye?"

"It may take a week or two. I have her reading my books and watching movies that just may pique her interest."

"I have a few books, too, that could help."

"Yours are too scientific, and would confuse her more than anything."

"How do you know that?"

"They confuse me." Kaye pushed her glasses to the tip of her nose, tightened her lips and gave him that 'over the top of the glasses, just because I know' kind of look. He sat back and said, "OK."

"Ya know, these people are big on photographs. I'll find some old images of us when we were children and turn them into photos." Professor Stevens said.

"That sounds like a good idea to me. I can find a frame for you to put them in; there are a plenty of reusable shops around here."

"Sure that can work, too."

"I'm not sure if I should frame them or put a group of them in an album," Kaye said.

"Dearie, I think that just might overwhelm her."

"Yeah, you're probably right."

"We have two days to be ready for her visit and you know there can be no pictures of me anywhere. Jacob knows me as his PawPaw, his eccentric missing marbles, great-grandfather."

Professor Stevens and Kaye plotted and planned the whole night. Brid woke them up from their comfortable chairs just a little past sun up, singing, "We gotta plan, we gotta plan."

"The bird's gotta go," Said Stevens as his eyes opened to Kaye's startled, almost-awake gaze. Brid repeated, "The bird's gotta go."

"No, she whispered, I'll put a cover over him, and he will go to sleep."

"Put him in the bedroom and let's get a radio or television for him to listen to all day then he can really be confused and no one will pay attention to him, especially when he starts singing those ads."

135

After a few days and later in that day Grace came over as planned and handed Kaye a bouquet of yellow flowers. "This is a lovely place, Kaye, how did you fix it up so quickly?"

"My friend came over and helped me."

"Why did you just up and move like that?"

"Oh, the owners didn't want the bird there," she said.

"What movers did you use? You have such delicate things and nothing got broken! "

"I don't know the name of the company...my friend set that all up for me."

"Oh, my, do I sense a long lost love or something here?"

"No, no, just a dear friend."

"Dear friends?"

"Yes, we've known each other forever, so to speak."

" Forever?"

"Yes, forever."

"Okay, I'll drop the subject."

"I'm okay, I'm k, I'm okay" said Brid from the other room. "We got a plan, we got a plan, we got a plan."

"What's that bird talking about now?"

"He's been watching the television and now repeats what he hears there constantly, I tell you, he's a mess."

"One Step Beyond, one step beyond," yelled Brid.

Grace said. "That's an old sci-fi show, remember that?"

"I think I've seen it a time or two, a long time ago."

"Well, let's see what this episode is about with all those books I've been reading and movies...you know, I'm beginning to believe there is more than we know and see in everyday life going on all around us."

"Why do you say that, Grace?"

"Some of the things I've been reading remind me of images and shadows I've seen since...well, as long as I can remember anything...That's why I named my cat Shadow. He just showed up one day and...well, you aren't going to believe this but...I hope you don't think I'm out of my mind or anything, but..."

Kaye looked at her hopefully wanting to blurt out who she is.

"I used to see shadows and things that no one else could see."

"Oh, what kind of things?"

"I'm sorry I said anything, you must think I'm a nut case, too"

"Oh no, I believe every word you said. I see things too, sometimes just flashes, and then sometimes real people and they vanish. I used to think I was stuck in daydreams."

"What happened? Did you tell anyone?"

"I searched for others like me, and knew that when the shadows and pictures and rustling occurred...and the others looked in the same direction I did, we had like minds or some call it kindred spirits," Kaye said.

"Is that why you found me?"

"No, you found me remember?"

"I was minding my own business, just sitting on the park bench when you came up to me chasing after your Shadow." They both laughed but were stopped by a chill in the air. They both felt it. Goose bumps appeared on their faces and arms.

Grace surveyed the room and began to recognize many of the items as hers. Still not fully grasping the whole scenario she touched and smelled her belongings.

"You know who my real parents are, don't you?"

Kaye maintained her composure and gave an affirmative nod. It took all the strength she had not to change her expression or say anything but rather to keep her eyebrows down, straight, even, and her lips held tightly together from the inside.

"Should I be afraid?" asked Grace.

"Oh, no, dear, I'm the one who's been afraid...afraid that you would not get to this point of wanting to know more about where you come from and who you are."

"Am I from someplace else? Another planet, perhaps?" She smiled and busted out laughing raucously. "Who am I? Jacob's Jenny?" she said sarcastically, remembering one of the movies Kaye had given her to watch.

Kaye smiled. "In a sense, yes. You are here because of his doing, but we don't know why or how and we don't believe he knows either. At least not consciously."

"You said 'We'...you mean there are more of you?"

"You say that like you're talking about roaches or rodents or something. We are all the same, its just that some have more...more mobility than others."

"Mobility? What does that mean?"

"I can show you better than tell you. Take a good look at the clock, remember what time it is right now." Kaye said to Grace. While Grace concentrated on the clock, Kaye was busy setting coordinates and trying to think of what to do next.

"If there were places...or anything you'd like to see in this whole wide world, from any time, what would it be?"

"Oh, I don't know."

"Is there nothing you want to see?"

"Well, what's your favorite place?" Grace asked Kaye

"My favorite place to go...is the ocean, to be sitting on the sand at five minutes before sunset." Kaye said as she fiddled with this small gadget on her wrist...then everything got smaller.

Suddenly they were marveling at a setting sun on the Pacific Ocean.

"What the hell happened?" asked Grace who now was beginning to realize her identity. They maintained their silence. "Why didn't you wait for me?" Lily asked.

"Wait for you?" said Kaye

"Yeah!" emphatically, Lily said, "you heard me. What happened to you with your 'I'll be back right away. Yeah, Right!'"

"Thank God, you know me, you're back." Kaye yelled, jumping up and down in the sand, rocking her feet back and forth heel to toe in the sand then kicking the sand in the air. Kaye filled Lily in on all that had happened all the way to this point, as much as she knew.

"There's renegade interference and we both got sucked into it. I got lost, too," said Kaye, "but in all the previous journeys I always left myself clues as to how to get home. One day I realized who I really was but didn't know how to get back to myself. I thought I'd die without ever finding anyone, or anyone ever finding me."

"So how did you find out how to get back?" A friend found me and immediately I was transformed, well almost immediately, and then we started looking for you."

"So you think Jacob is a part of this?"

"It may or may not be him, but it is closely attached to him."

"I know he loves Grace—well, me, as Grace,"

"But I really think we should get rid of her," Kaye said.

"You mean kill her off?"

"Yeah, how you wanna go?" said Kaye

Lily thought for a moment, "Quickly."

"How?"

"Accident."

"What kind?"

"Auto."

"Need to get anything from home to take with you?"

"No, I can always come back if I want. If I think of something, I'll get it later." There was a sudden light chill around them, like waking up to the touch of a butterfly. Kaye pressed enter on the TTC and the chill followed them.

"If we get lost again, how do I find you?" asked Lily.

"Grocery store, like before—there will always be grocery stores, or markets with food. When you walk in the door or area of where they are selling food, you will know if I'm around. If you check the vegetable bins and look for out of place candy canes. And I'll look for out of place vegetables."

Lily kind of pouted and said, "You've got to be more specific than that."

"Ok, Ok, how about String beans, again? I will leave them where the candy canes should be and you leave the string beans with the candy canes. Then we meet or wait, watch for each other on the east side of the structure. And don't forget to leave notes."

"Deal?"

"Deal."

Chapter 23

"First, Kaye, there's something I need to know."

"What's that?'

"What happened to the whole world after the Twenty-first century? Not waiting for an answer, Lily continued, "I mean the here and now is beautiful, I just don't understand."

Kaye began, reluctantly. "Well, it seems that every few thousand years there is a complete overhaul of thinking. Some of it you can readily see from decade to decade. There is a twist here and another one there. Groups of people searching for any measurement of sameness so that they can justify their allegiance, then two, three decades, or even a century later their new justification is power over the other."

"Why did that happen, when there's an ample supply of everything for the taking?"

Kaye rested the heel of her hand on her knee. "Maybe I should rephrase that," as she waved her hand back and forth like she was erasing an imaginary chalkboard. "It's also about control. You see, its not enough for some of these people here to have 'enough' but they also have to control everyone else's 'enough.'

Lily interrupted, saying, "I still don't understand..."

"Good, that means you know what you don't know." Kaye noticed Lily's shoulders tighten and jaw became ridged.

"I'm not putting you down or anything, its just that...remember when you read about the different ages that the people on planet earth have endured?"

"Yeah, but what has that got to do with power and control?"

"Everything! There was the ice age, then the stone age, then agricultural then, Industrial then technological or informational age."

"But what does that have to do with these people now?"

"Darling, it's another Pandora's box, paradigm shift, or...let's say it's Adam and Eve with the forbidden fruit. Everything was or had been in God's perfect harmony, you remember reading that don't you?"

"Yes, I do."

"When that information age began, it influenced the entire globe."

"When exactly did that start?"

"It was always there, it just took the right set of events and circumstances to reveal itself. You see, in the early-to-mid 1900's there was a new revelation of thought, ideas and inventions, which found its premise in the century before, like the airplane, then Jet, then Stealth up until now, where none of that is necessary.

This global travel brought about other unnecessary problems that had to be worked through society, understanding and love. Many didn't reach this plateau, because, they thought it was their mission, to own every damn thing. All this stuff here is just stuff. It eventually rots and blows away. You see, people were entrusted by God to care for all that He gave them, no all of us."

"And they didn't use them, right?" Lily tried to confirm.

"People, things, possessions, stuff...everything was misused! Everything! Misused! So, whenever the planet reaches this realm of decadence, things fall apart and begin to deteriorate, and only then do we see how everything is interconnected.

The race to outer space culminated in all out competition. This began publicly only after entities, from another planet, arrived here somewhere back in the mid 1900s. There were many before then, but they did not share that information worldwide. After that it took more than twenty years for the earth to send a group to the moon where they landed safely and could walk around. They didn't find any life forces there because in their arrogance, they were looking for people who looked like themselves or those other races who landed here on earth before. 1947, I think it was."

"But how does that affect this time and place?" Lily asked, "I mean the missing information where did it go."

"Greed and paranoia go a long way, and people wanted to store more and more information externally. But we were, made in God's image meaning that we are to go within for all information, for recall, for teaching generations. Everything is implanted in us from our beginning. The people did not grow weaker and wiser; just weaker." Kaye said.

The invention of computers was not new to man, it was just new to those who discovered it then. It actually started with the abacus. But all the technology, energy forces and such had always been. There is nothing new under the sun, only changes in forms of the elements. God called everything into being and that's all there was and is. Now the manual for life says, 'All things were made by Him; and without Him was not anything made that was made. He made everything in six days then rested. So what does that tell you?" Kaye asked.

"I'm not sure except that we're here now and—-"

Kaye stopped her. "This earth and everything in it was made to sustain itself and evolve; revolve but always continue. Nothing ever truly dies here. It just becomes something with a different purpose." Kaye stretched out in the sand for a time.

They stared at the water moving towards them and stopping on its own.

"So let me get back to technology and computers...these things began to be relied upon for everything from making simple calculations to nuclear warfare. Then every so often, a glitch infected the computer's memory and functions giving the idea to some of the controlling greedy humans to make those very problems with computer malfunctions on their command, ergo—control! Which could also be translated into more money, greed. In this time viruses that suddenly 'attacked' computers, then suddenly anti virus fixit applications appeared...more money. There are no coincidences. Remember that."

Lily didn't remember and shook her head no.

"When the network of computers began to talk to each other it meant people didn't have to. That's another breakdown. The computers stored information that should have been stored in our brains, so we relied on them more and more. It got to the point that the computers no longer store information within their machines, but rather places in the air. At first computers, needed massive amounts of space, energy and people, but within a few years there were computers in almost every home. People carried them around in little satchels, then they become the size of an ink pen without the hardware of a keyboard, so people just lit them up to throw an image, whenever they wanted to use it."

"Didn't they have to have clearance to operate them?" Lily questioned.

"No, just the resources to buy and maintain them, during these days many, in high authority used the phrase 'there are the haves and the have mores, 'those who revealed their greed and control, and those who lived their purpose, as given, and those who suffered unmercifully."

"So how did that matter?"

STRING BEANS & CANDY CANES

"All areas of the globe contained some of the greedy controlling forces that over burdened the planet, always wanting more and more and better and bigger...until, the natural resources were almost totally depleted. At that point, the Earth began to rebel. There were mammoth storms that wiped out entire countries. And—

"What kind of storms?"

"Hurricanes, tsunamis, floods and epidemics. The people had used up so many trees for making houses and furniture, hoarding some of them that promised medical cures...and, too, the trees could no longer hold the ground because they could no longer link their roots.

These diseases took over and many were unable to find medicines because of greed. Then there were those who planted the diseases to annihilate certain groups of people, but that came back to haunt them because the diseases grew wild and many who acquired the diseases were not the unintentional targets."

"But even with all that, how did we get to now, in our century? Our atmosphere controlled by machines, even our personal environment is controlled. Whose plan was that?"

"That's a man-made plan to control every movement of creatures and plants."

Lily's hands slowly slid to her knees and rested as her face moved up to enjoy the clarity of the evening sky. "Why do I remember riding past a rolling river?" She paused not really waiting for an answer but tying to connect all the scenarios.

".... but it was not Jacob." Kay announced.

"What'd you say? I'm sorry, my mind was someplace else."

"You were in that environment, not by your choice, but...how do I say this? Kidnapped by the person we have to watch out for! All this time, I thought the danger was Jacob. Now I know it's someone else and I've got to find him before something else happens and we can't find each other, forever.

The monster's not sure where in time he is, but if you summons Jacob to our time again, he will follow him and get to you."

"Who is the 'he' we you are talking about?"

"...not sure, but you may know. Is there anyplace in your house that he keeps secret?"

"No."

"Is there anyplace in the house that you can't go?"

"No, but there is a place I don't go."

"Why?"

"It's cold and eerie, kind of spooky, ya know?"

"What's in the place?"

"Jacob's old military stuff."

"Outside or in?"

"It's a closet in the basement."

"Does he talk about anyone from his military time?"

"Not really. But sometimes he has nightmares and mentions someone named Baxter."

"Does he ever talk about this Baxter?"

"Once I asked him who it was and he looked at me like he'd seen a ghost and his skin turned gray—-you know, I didn't push further after that."

"Did he tell you anything?"

"He just said the incident was one of the horrors of war and please don't ask him about it and that he wasn't yet ready to talk about it. He wouldn't even say the man's name; he just said that it was a friend that died when he didn't have to."

"Are you ready to go?" Kaye asked.

"Can I ask him to come with me?"

"Now, what did I just say to you?"

Lily didn't answer.

"Not yet, you're not safe here now." Kaye repeated

"Not safe?"

"I think the demon is getting to you through Jacob."

"The demon?"

"Like I said earlier, you were kidnapped and so was I. He's going to unleash more havoc on the world and kill as many of the living as he can. When he's finished only a remnant of the population will be left. As I said before, 'total control and greed. Baxter and his group of thieves want to lengthen their days to forever! That's what they're trying to do."

They decided to just stay there and continued to lay in the warm sand and watch the night's sky.

Chapter 24

Kaye drove faster and faster, making sure no innocent bystander would be pulled into their escape when she hit the curve going past the river at 90 miles per hour. Just before the car hit the water she pushed enter and one on-looker witnessed them fly out of the car.

It was an intense struggle to get back into their own time. The entity was following them. Lily knew it wasn't Jacob, but she had felt this same spirit around in her own house. Thoughts came rushing at her and she remembered it came from the area where Jacob kept his old military stuff, only certain times of the day.

Kaye and Lily locked arms and held on back to back. They knew that in order to survive they could not let go of each other. Lily's hand found Kaye's wrist and she remembered there was an escape button on the TTC so she pressed it and held it down. They landed back in the sand at sunset.

Meanwhile, Jacob opened his front door and two police officers told him that his wife, Grace, had been in an accident and there was an aquatic search team trying to find her and her friend Kaye in the river where the car plummeted.

"I know who that spirit belongs to." Lily said.

"Me too." Said Kaye.

"All this time I could have sworn it was Jacob, but wow! Who'd have thought?"

"He's been carrying around that spirit because of the guilt he felt, and it isn't even his to carry."

"We all hang onto garbage that begins to cling to us like we need it, while we justify its right to be. All the while it is choking our spirit and joy and confiscates our time."

"Why was Jacob hanging on to that monster?"

"He believed he was responsible for his death."

"But he wasn't. I saw it and now I know why, if Jacob had died that night, Baxter would have been let loose on the whole society, and there's no telling what havoc or how many lives and spirits could have been damaged. Baxter kept Jacob in that guilt mindset so that Jacob would go back and reset the traps to change his fate. So he could gain in power and influence over more and more souls. Some old beliefs, spirits, dogs and monsters need to just lay down and die, but individually we have to realize that we must let them go and leave them be."

"Yeah, like taking out the garbage," Lily said.

"No, its more like completely destroying the garbage...otherwise some kind sweet soul may bring it back from the dump."

"So now how do we get back to our own selves?"

"Well, we have to make sure we know where our old selves are. There's another piece of you with the old lady Kaye; they think I'm senile, and your new self is the one who went back and exposed us to Jacob. They are a bit upset with you, but I ain't mad at you."

"Yes, it was me, but I didn't know about Baxter at the time."

"So now, where are you going? Coming back home for a while?" asked Kaye.

"Yes, for a little while. Should I go back to where I left last time?"

"Well, maybe you should view the one's of you we brought back just to see what they've been up to. Gather yourself together, girl. If you do that, all of you will be in one spot."

"But what about all that's happened?" said Lily.

"Oh that's just about all smoothed out, anyway."

"What about that Baxter spirit and those others? Will he continue to haunt Jacob? Is he still running lose?"

" We can not control all of those others because there are millions."

"Stevens and Benny took care of that...I mean those that we encountered."

"Can I ask how?" asked Lily.

"Give it some time, okay?"

"Ok, ok, ok, by the way where is Brid?" With a great big smile, Lily asked, "What happened to him?"

"Ya know that it was Brid and Shadow who found me for you, and I guess all of us."

"He's at home, somewhat confused but he will be fine, okay, okay, okay? He was Hannah's bird, she will care for him."

"She's a very old soul."

"She was able to keep all her angels, too."

"Now she's really got some traveling secrets."

"You know, Hannah is the one who kinda spilled the beans, don't you think?"

"No, how?"

"Her inference to time travel without really saying anything set Jacob off, when they were getting ready for a family outing, I think right then he was looking for you...Lily, not Grace."

"Oh yeah?" Lily stood up and hit the sand from her clothes. Kaye could see she was readying herself to go.

"So which home are you going to visit first?"

"Well, I think I should check into my original spot. I need to see about something."

Kaye stood, with a bit of a smirky kind of smile. "You think he's there?"

"I've a few places to check things out."

"Like…?"

"Oh here and there. But I'll see you back home real soon."

Then there was nothing, not even footprints.

Chapter 25

Now at the same time Kaye was introducing Lily back to her real self, Stevens was trying to set things right with Jacob. He thought about all the things Jacob had been doing lately. *That bar*, he thought. *Maybe there was someone there that knows something.*

The place to go when you didn't want to impress anyone, or just to sit and have a drink and be around others who were in that same funky frame of mind was called The Dive. Jacob had become a regular there.

Stevens and Ben sat in that dimly lit, smoke-filled, beer joint for about 15 to 20 minutes before a waitress in hot pants approached their table.

"Legs, haven't seen you in quite a while, how's it going?"

"What you guys come in here for? I told you my name ain't Legs, you ole coot." She handed them the menu and walked away. Ben and Stevens watched her even after she was out of their range of vision. They sat in silence staring at the table, and throwing quick glances around the room. Ben tapped his fingernail on the table, irritating the hell out of Stevens. Stevens rock back and forth in his chair as if he were somewhere outside on a back porch, in a hand made wicker and wood rocking chair, his chair.

They were both somewhat startled when "Y'all ready to order?' she said as she approached their table.

"Not yet. Has Jacob been in here lately?" asked Ben.

"Scotch and soda."

"Same for me"

"Yeah, he was here first by himself then some strange-looking guy came in and started talking to him, he acted like he knew him well."

"When was that?"

"Last Thursday, 'bout this time."

"What do you mean, 'strange'?"

"Well, I don't think he's from around here, but he looked old then young all at the same time."

"How so?"

"I mean, he wasn't even wearing the same clothes some time when I looked over at their table, Jacob started out just sitting at the bar...hold on, I'll be right back."

She left to serve another customer and Ben said, "He's one of the others trying to find a way to survive through Jacob."

"I'm checking this out for a second," Stevens disappeared then reappeared instantly. "He's alright for now." Stevens said. "I got him home into bed and then put the light around him. They can't get to him for a while."

"Like I was saying" the waitress started the conversation right where she left to go wait on another table. "The second guy just sort of moved on next to him and they got a table. It seemed like they knew each other."

She took a deep breath and looked around to see if anybody else wanted something. " That other guy kept on getting more beer but he didn't seem to be drinking any, just Jacob. They got some sammitches, but before I served them they were talking about something real secret because they were both looking down at the table and not talking as loud as at first, ya know what I'm saying?"

"Yeah," Stevens and Ben said at the same time.

"Well anyway, they were here almost to closing time, just talking real serious like, and I think Jacob went to sleep a time or two."

"How's that?"

"He had his hand on his forehead and over one eye. That's when that other guy would go over to the Juke and put money in it...he played a lot of old tunes."

"What else?"

"He went to the bathroom a lot, but once he was there a long time. A man came out and I asked him if the guy was in there asleep, he said, there wasn't anybody there but him. Right then, that guy who was sitting with Jacob came out of the restroom. Strange."

"Did you know that other man who came out of the restroom?"

"He looked familiar, but I can't say I know who he is. But you know there was one thing that was kinda funny, not the laughing kinda funny, but the weird kind...and that's when they left, Jacob and the man he was talking with, well, the man left all his food. I mean the bag was there and the entire sammitch, too. I went out the door after him and it was like he just disappeared. He sure got away from here fast. That other man that I told you 'bout came out of the restroom, well, he was across the street at the bus stop.

Jacob, on the other hand, was two sheets to the wind and was roaming around, looking for his car. I thought that when he found it, he'd just sit there and go to sleep. I never seen him drink that much before. But when I got off work an hour later, I looked for him and his car was gone."

"Has he been in here since then? Jacob, that is?"

"Naw, I ain't seen him."

"What about the other two men?"

"I haven't seen them anymore either. Why you asking me all these questions? Did Jacob get robbed or something that night?" she asked.

"Well, Jacob lost his wallet and we're just trying to help him trace his tracks," Ben lied, "He's embarrassed so don't tell him we told you, okay?"

"Sure, sure, give me your card and if either of those men come back I'll call you. That second man was creepy, I think he peed on hisself, too."

"Why do you think that?"

"His shoes were soaking wet." she replied.

Ben and Stevens disappeared, leaving the waitress there, then returned before the next tick of time. Their quick travel took them to the street on the night in question; they must have missed the time because no one was there, outside the bar.

She looked up, questionably as she was just gone away in her mind for a moment. "I must get back to work now, but if I can get you anything, I'd be glad to. Wine, beer, sammitch?"

They thanked her with a good-sized tip and left. Without saying a word both knew that they were going to 'last week' and find out who those mysterious familiars were.

Chapter 26

Ben saw them first, right after Jacob began roaming the parking lot. Ben cloaked himself in the building's shadow watched and listened. He signaled a warning so Stevens landed quietly behind Ben. They looked up as a cat dashed though the parking lot right in front of the strange men, so they in turn relaxed their defenses.

Stevens and Ben saw a chance right then to summons Cora and Kaye, and so they did. Lily showed up with them; the real, back-to-her-senses, Lily. The 'Others' were Chandler, Baxter and a young Hispanic guy they called Tony. Stevens wondered how Tony could be involved.

The group surrounded the others and identified all their vulnerabilities and then on signal wrapped their own time around them. The others struggling to reach their weapons did not realize that Stevens and his crew had already annihilated their ability to hold anything solid. In keeping with their plan they knew that the immediate next step was to synchronized their TTCs. They let the others know, in no uncertain terms, that they were destroyed. They hurled them into the earth's core, a mantle of burning molting rock where they would disintegrate and be gone forever—even their souls.

The five of them held their breath until silence was absolute. No one wanted to break the calm. So to be sure, they

STRING BEANS & CANDY CANES

continued to wait. They felt a ripple radiating under their feet through the concrete. One had perhaps broken loose but was unable to free himself, so he'd have to live with the worms for a while. There was no one left to free him. They weren't sure which one it was, so they could be looking out for Chandler, Baxter or Tony.

A five-person sigh filled the area as they huddled together.

Hot Pants came running out of the Bar. "Did anybody get hurt?" They looked at her wild, frightened eyes like she'd spoken a language they'd never heard.

"No, why would you ask that?" said Stevens.

"Well, we, ah, I heard a loud noise like something had crashed." She looked around and just missed seeing the last piece of the sidewalk mend itself.

"Perhaps we were taking too loud. I'm sorry if we disturbed anything."

"Now Stevens, go ahead and tell her that you're the one who hit that pole," chimed in Ben.

They turned to see an old car with its right fender smashed into a telephone pole a few feet away.

"I don't think we should stop to get another drink, you've had enough," Ben continued.

Stevens turned around and shouted in a slurred "Legs!"

" Oh, it's you. I should have known you were a drunk, too, you ole coot. It felt like a little earthquake on the inside, even the glasses was shaking in there."

"No one's hurt. We'd better get him home."

"Yeah, that old coot's gonna kill somebody." She walked back into the club.

They all walked to the car that so conveniently appeared, waited for the coast to be clear and left together with the auto in tow.

"There is one more of them out there, that's gonna try to get back here, you know," Said Ben.

"I think its that little guy, not one of the brothers, ah, Tony," replied Stevens.

"Yes, but we will be waiting. He will try to pick us off one by one, so we either all have to stick together, or find a way to stop his efforts now." Said Kaye.

The group went back to their own times, a place that they didn't think any of the three knew how to get. They replenished and hydrated their bodies, bathed and rested.

Lily redrafted her plan to invite Jacob to her time while Cora and Kaye had other things to do.

Stevens and Ben decided to wait for the attack that was soon to come.

They sent Jacob to the mountain cabin, a place he needed to be. He still hadn't mastered time-travel and he was in a place that the renegades didn't expect. Then, Ben and Stevens took over his house and time. Shadow sat quietly in the far corner watching them as they straightened the place for their comfort. "What's your game man, poker or chess?" Stevens asked.

"Let's do both, Ben. What's your pleasure; scotch, rum, vodka, bourbon, wine or beer?"

"Your grandson is well stocked, huh? We can start with scotch."

"Cool beans! When that scoundrel we sent to hell arrives, we will send him back to the mantle with his cronies or out to the farthest star dust particle."

They waited and drank and laughed, playing poker and chess at the same time. The stranger came, but they were ready for him.

It didn't take much because every entry was trapped. When Tony arrived, he carried the spirit of Baxter. He was immobilized immediately, but put up a hell of a fight. When their TTCs rays struck him, he descended…at first, but there was interference of some sort.

"I think they knew we'd be here, it's a good thing we knew about his shield. He's blocking for Baxter's time. He's about to go back with the 'Others' now, this time forever. The energy in the house took over and the floors moved upward, and the air lifted everything.

"Plan B." They both pushed enter and the roof blew off and two of the walls imploded and Ben and Stevens stood there watching Tony, with Baxter's spirit attached to him, leave the planet in perpetuity.

Chapter 27

After several days, or years, or centuries, however you want to think of it many miles away, Lily walked the floor of her apartment. She finally decided that she would go back one more time to see what happened to Jacob and why he had not come before now. She had been patient, knowing that there was a lot for him to deal with, and he was really just caught up in his job, and school, and Grace and...*Stop making excuses*...she told herself. *He hasn't come so—go see why*. She thought about the harsh blow it must have been to think that his wife had been killed. To tell the truth, she missed him because now she remembered everything.

Lily had confided in Professor Stevens how many times she had gone back to the Twentieth century to see Professor Nobel. How she found an ancient automobile, restored it then took it with her to the oldest section of the city where she actually drove it around. His eyebrows rose to meet on his forehead when she told him this, but he did not say anything. He waived to her in a motion to continue as he listened to all that had happened. She finally told him about Jacob using the TTC to go back in time just enough to see her drive away in the car. Professor Stevens had not chastised her but warned her to be careful.

"There are forces that would restrict all time travel." he said. "Just be careful of where and when you go. And leave a message someplace of where you are, just in case you encounter trouble. After that Lily left his office and waited patiently these last two weeks for Jacob to arrive and…and what? *What am I expecting from him?* She asked herself.

Lily could not bring herself to recognize the emotional tie she had to an ancient, long dead, history professor named Jacob Nobel. She could not explain it to herself or to any one that in recent months, since she started this project, said she had changed. The people she knew accused her of being different in some way, of almost being a different person. Lily was different in more ways than she even knew. But now she knew why.

Lily sat back and relaxed for a while in her comfy antique chair. The chair was much too large; and nobody used that much space anymore for just one piece of furniture. Reflecting on all that happened during the last few months, the years she'd spanned, Lily realized that she did have strength, courage and knowledge. Not just because of the King Tut tomb and the kidnapping but in all she was. She Survived. Lily knew many of the 'whys' 'what for's,' and 'how comes.' But those were all the tangible things, and there was one area she hadn't quite figured out. The 'why me.'

People of old baffled her mostly, especially their coveting nature. The wanting something someone else had, or stealing it, asking for it, copying it, ridiculing it or trying to purchase it was how they got what they wanted. This behavior permeated through all the times she had experienced. She wondered why the energy of those who labored and were proud of their accomplishments never became an item of envy, or a trend. As she looked up, the light from outside crossed the room and rested on the cello in the corner. She smiled, sauntered from her reclining next to the cello and then rested her elbows on her knees. She just wanted to think, but found herself just cradling the cello.

Jacob looked at the clock on the wall near the fireplace: 8:45 PM. He opened the TTC and punched in the coordinates for his next journey. He set the TTC for auto return, just in case something should happen. He could change it if need be. He was a little apprehensive: the future, so far in the future. This would all be unfamiliar territory. He picked up the letter and book, looked around the room one more time and then at the clock again 8:47 PM. He picked up the TTC and pushed the enter button. He looked down at Shadow, as he seemed to get smaller and smaller, then everything was dark and the familiar movement once again gave him the queasy feeling in his stomach.

Jacob's next moment found him standing in Lily's home. She stood next to a window…suddenly he remembered what he saw early one morning in his living room, the next second she was gone and he thought it was his imagination or a leftover dream. But that was so long ago, even before The Point. It was she, and it was also her in the car. Neither spoke. They each waited for the other to begin, even though both had anxiously awaited this very second.

Then PawPaw was there and Jacob gasped.

Lily said to Professor Stevens "What are you doing here?"

He took Lily by the hand and left Jacob standing there in amazement. "PawPaw?" he yelled.

"Go home!" said Stevens

Jacob stood there alone in the room. "What the hell happened?" he asked out loud. "Anybody there? Anybody here?"

Jacob stood frozen in thought and body as all the events of this last half-year came gushing through his mind and body. In a great shiver, the subtle comments, glances and dismissed sightings of movement and shadows, things and people, began to piece themselves into a brand new paradigm.

Was that a TTC Ben stuck so quickly in his desk drawer? And PawPaw…He knows about all this? He's a part of it? Who else?

What does all this have to do with me? What do they want with me? Why the hell am I here? Where is Grace really? Was she a part of this too? His thoughts ran wild. He quickly left.

There was something he had to find out, so he began to look at all his childhood photographs. He paid particular attention to the pictures that showed his neck. None in his early years revealed a birthmark, tattoo or scar. It appeared mysteriously in pictures taken in his teens. It looked like a question mark...or was it a candy cane; there were diagonal stripes on it. He had seen that same kind of mark on different things in his own home after Kaye turned up. So he decided he'd go back to earlier times.

"I've been waiting for you," she broke the silence. He was still speechless. "I know I owe you an explanation," she continued, "but I don't really know where to begin." Jacob tried to catch his breath as he backed away into the wall behind. His heart pounded uncontrollably and his stomach turned into knots. *Is this real?* He thought. He saw a picture of himself on a table, the same picture that was on the back cover of his book. "Won't you say hello?' she asked.

"Uhm, ah, hello," he stammered. More silence filled the room. Her eyes fixed on his every motion, he noticed and almost, matter of fact said, trying to keep all emotion out of his voice, even though he didn't want her to get closer because he felt his shoes were cemented to the floor and he couldn't move.

"Hello, Cob," she said. His brows met mid forehead as he wondered where she came up with that name.

"The first time I met you, we were in line to start school, we couldn't have been much older than 5 years old. Your sweater was on crooked and covered the first two letters of your name, just like now." He looked down at his chest and saw that his scarf did indeed cover part of his name. She knew exactly what he was thinking and answered; "We have run into and out of each other's lives since then. But because of the controversy caused by your actions, my access to you was to be limited. Quite naturally, I felt that there was a part in you that was redeemable and that's why I tried so hard to stay in your life."

"So I wasn't just imagining things, when I thought I saw someone just out of the corner of my eye? Or felt a touch on my shoulder, or something brush against me?"

"Sometimes it was I, sometimes others."

"Have you been waiting long?" He forced from his lips.

"Only a century or two...or maybe three," she giggled, remembering the giggle he longed to hear from her before. Hearing that sound, his throat tried to hold back a hollow sob, his eyes filled with water, and his heart hurt. "Who the hell are you?" he asked almost in a rage.

She walked toward him and realized he could not back away even though he wanted to run, but he was more curious than fearful. "Please, it's really ok. Sit down, I need to answer all your whys." He sat down, looked into her eyes and waited for her words to fill in all the missing places.

"Why me? " he said.

"Perhaps you should ask a member of your family." she responded.

He gasped trying not to show any emotion—not surprise, shock, concern, curiously, or...*Why hadn't anyone told him about PawPaw?*

"You've had a rough six months, especially the last 72 hours."

"Oh, yes, in spades, a rough couple three days," he answered.

"Would you like some nourishment to replenish your system?"

He stared at her, waiting for a laugh or a continuation of the sentence. "Don't we just eat food anymore?" *What's this 'replenish your system crap?* he thought but said with a half smile, "What do you mean?"

"Give me your hand," she continued, "I'll show you." She placed his hand on a lighted contraption and a screen popped up that identified a scanning of his entire body's functions. "Oh! You are in need of quite a bit of nourishment, and you've got too much of some. Let's see how close we can get you into balance." Goose bumps traveled through him and there was a slight tingling in his hands that lay on the lighted box. "What is this? I am not going to be your experiment! Is that what I've gotten myself into?"

"Really, this is not experimentation; we can replenish ourselves quite easily without eating flesh or foliage," said Lily and Jacob's eyebrows reached upward to meet his hairline and his eyes remained as big as light bulbs. "Our bodies are made up of minerals exactly as in the soil, so we take from the soil and give back to it. Really, it's much more efficient than the old way."

"During this scan all our cells are scanned and repaired in this process. Here, I'll show you." She stepped into what appeared to be a closet, put her feet into some funny looking slippers and a red, then yellow, then brown, then white light traveled from the bottom of her feet to the top of her head. Her eyes remained closed. She took a deep breath, opened her eyes and smiled. "See, it didn't kill me. It's easy, now what about you?"

There go those goose bumps again, he thought. "I don't know about this."

"Shall we go back to your time, then? You do need to drink some water and you also need some fundamental minerals back in your system."

"Alright, I will try just about anything once." He stepped in. "Hey that feels pretty good, but did you guys also get rid of the toilet, too, when these changes were made? Since you now know about the make-up of my system, I guess you know I have to" she held up her hand as if to say, "stop" and pointed to another door. "Has this changed, too? I mean, do I have to stand on my head or something?"

She laughed out loud and for a second Jacob heard and smelled, saw and felt Grace.

"Just go in and you'll know what to do." she quipped.

"Why me?" he asked. "Why'd you pick me?"

"I didn't exactly pick you," Lily started. "When you were much younger, still in your teen years in fact, we were re-introduced and we, you and I, ran into each other several times while traveling. It was determined by the 'Powers' that you were not yet ready to know more about our 23rd century technology."

"But," she paused. "I..." She stopped and stared into the air.

The silence caused Jacob to tighten his fists and hold his breath almost til he felt he would burst. "Alright, alright," he said when he gained some of his composure. "Please go on. Tell me more," he prodded.

"I want to be perfectly honest with you," she said.

"Please," he said.

They both stood there, spellbound, neither knowing where to go from here.

Jacob decided to go back home, to his time. He wouldn't admit it, but this stuff was too strange for him to hold onto. *We are just two disconnected souls,* he thought. However, he continued to investigate different areas of the world, experiment in different times, and eventually going back to that very same conversation he had with Lily.

He even found that he and Pawpaw (a.k.a. Professor Stevens) could communicate now. They made a pact that neither of them would interfere in the workings of the world, except with the approval of the "Powers.' Jacob found that out-of-the-way resting place again, that Ben told him about. It was Benny and Pawpaw's hideaway when the world was acting up.

Chapter 28

Jacob stood on the porch looking out over the valley. He was miles away from the nearest town and he was sure no one knew he was there. The snow was still eight to 20 feet deep and likely to last until at least June, maybe even July. There was only one route to this cabin and it closed down after the first couple of snowfalls. There was virtually no access, aside from hiking up to the 10,000 foot level in snowshoes, so Jacob knew he wasn't likely to be surprised by guests just passing through. A person had to make a deliberate, coordinated effort to reach him there. The remote place in the Alps was awesome. Only time travelers like himself could find him.

The cabin actually belonged to PawPaw and Benny and his father who had been lost long ago. They had mysteriously acquired it though the centuries, and everyday men used it for hunting in the twentieth century. Jacob had come there many times as a kid with PawPaw and his father. It was so high that many of the animals were too far below the snowline to even see. He liked it, though, the solitude, the view. *Top of the world*, he thought.

He tugged on the collar of his jacket pulling it up around his ears and his cap lower below his ears. The wind blew constantly here. Now there was just a slight breeze, but he knew that the evening would bring stronger winds. He would light a fire and think of all that had happened to him.

"It's been a year now, and I do believe I've lost my mind."
He spoke to the fire. He thought of Fishers Point and where
it had all started for him. It seemed like ages ago, but in
actuality, it had only been a year. He went back over the
sequence of events in his mind and could not help thinking
of the catalyst of this all: Grace. Why was she used and why did
she have to die? At least the spirit of her died and he couldn't
find that spirit he loved.

He made more notes about what, and who, he had seen
during this whole ordeal. He had enough material for several
books by now. He wondered, are *there more books I have
written?*

It had been difficult getting the people of the future to let
him keep his material. He argued in their informal hearings
for keeping his notes. They had put him through a lot, but he
knew all along that they would. *I guess this was a part of history,
too,* he thought.

*Finally, Lily. Who was she really? There was so much of her
that was like Grace. The way she wore her hair. The way she
signed her name, her expressions, and the little things she said and
the way she joked. It was like having Grace back, but she was not
Grace at all. She was a totally different person.* These thoughts
came crashing through his mind all at once.

He could no longer go back to their times together and
relive them; it was too painful. He turned and walked back
into the cabin. He lit a fire and poured himself a drink as tall
as he could make it.

It sounded like a whisper, if he hadn't known what to
expect. He continued staring at the dancing flames in the
hearth, acting as though he'd never heard it. Lily appeared out
of nowhere, out of time. She slipped her hand into his and
gave it a gentle squeeze.

"Hello," she said. "Have you been waiting long?"

He stared for what seemed twice as long as forever and answered, "of course, but you know that. All my life, actually."

Lily told him of all that had happened, and they sat together staring at the floor and then back at the fire dancing in the hearth. "I've loved you forever and then some," their spirits sang.

"Didn't you remember me as your husband for all that time we were together?" He was now ready for the answers to all the questions he had, but was afraid to hear. "Did you remember loving me and our promises to each other?" he pleaded.

"Partially." She answered in hesitant sigh. "Now its like a high alert fog. I find you in my dreams and sometimes try to go back there to our beginning; but, when I get there, it's not the way I remember it, so I stopped going there. I don't want my heart to hurt anymore. Everything is like someone else's daydream, and I'm a spectator."

"I don't want that either. Not for either of us. But, you could have told me before; before I thought you were dead. You could have saved me that sorrow and anguish."

"Really, I am dead to that time. But as you now know, I kept going back there just to learn about who you were to me. I didn't understand the Grace person you remember. Her mind wasn't real to me. She only held the knowledge of the time she was left there—and me, well I have 300 more years that I know and each time I was there I felt trapped."

Jacob couldn't hold back anymore, "You know I love you?"

She didn't answer, just continued her gaze at the fire dance.

"Well?" he asked.

"Yes." She finally said.

"And?" he asked.

"Why do you think I kept going back there? I was looking for a lost love; and I did ask if I could bring you forward with me."

"So, why didn't you? I mean before my heart broke in sorrow when I though you were dead?" he demanded to know in this heart breaking, again, plea.

"The powers said no." she watched the ashes drop down to the floor from the flames. "But I came back, time and time again to try to figure out what to do. What I wanted to do. So I waited until the times for both of us were right. But I had no idea what was lurking around either of us. I loved you even long before we ran into each other that day at your university. It seems like your essence has always been one with mine. I love you, your soul, your spirit your essence, your body—for always." She stopped and moved closer to his side and placed her arm around him.

"I've always loved you, too." He almost whispered, and his arm moved to embrace her. They watched the fire as they danced to the fire's song. In that one night while the fire danced in rhythm with their hearts, they wandered through each happy time that either of them remembered and held onto the memories and feelings they stirred. They examined their identical scars, his beneath his ear and hers above an ankle. They found that threshold and kept that very second tucked away in the tiny secret places their hearts and minds reserved for only each other.

"Jacob, I must tell you that somewhere there can be another glitch in our times and we could get lost." She said kind of matter of fact.

"How can we keep that from happening?" he wanted to know. "You know more about these things than I do, right now." He continued.

"Remember those god awful tasting flowers we tasted back when we saw each other as children? What do you bet your PawPaw and Kaye didn't have something to do with that?"

"I know he did." Jacob chimed right in. "Yes, I remember how hard I searched for something pretty for you only to find them bitter and..."

"I know, I know." She stopped him. "People will always have a place to gather or purchase food, right?"

"Right." He answered.

"OK, if either of us gets lost, let's leave some of those yellow petals in stores or markets in bins that sell or hold string beans or candy canes. No one will know but us." She remembered how Kaye had found her, but doesn't remember ever leaving those clues for her. But now this thought was in his mind.

In their embrace to seal their agreement with a kiss, he whispered, "Let's go find a place that's just for us."

Lily looked into Jacob's eyes and touching his lips with hers said, "why not right here?"

And they remained while the fire's dance stayed in rhythm with their souls.

Chapter 29

Hannah walked past the window just then. Jacob and Lily didn't look up to see the flutter by the pane or the change in shape of the sun's pattern on the floor. She moved on but had taken notice of all that had gone on, and quietly put back the things that were disturbed. The quartz rock that Lily had broken: How dare she just move that to her own liking," said Hannah. She waited though, until Lily forgot she had it, there was so much utter clutter all around her, anyway.

Lily's surroundings and her thoughts and other issues...just clutter. But Hannah knew that it might be reclaimed again for a foot massage or a vigorous back rub; or maybe even a weapon, for now it was Hannah's. The silk cloth gave others much pleasure and it never wore thin...amazing! The pig went back and fed a family instead of a tiger.

Hannah had been there all along and not that she absolutely knew the outcome, well completely, that is, but most of the information was there. She watched all the babies and knew who they were and some of their purposes. She wanted to make sure she could make things right. She dropped hints to the children when she mixed with them. They didn't really notice her because of their interest in the bird that always sat just behind her ear and the cat that looked like midnight but was as playful as a puppy. She shared comfort words when the children cried, so the next thing they knew, they were not crying anymore but rather lost in a good thought. Then she would go on to the next place she was supposed to be.

Her given name was Abira Hannah, which meant, Strong Goddess of Life, but everyone just called her Hannah most of the time. She had an old soul and didn't care much for attention, but when anyone saw her, she knew she was supposed to spend time with them and to tell that person something they needed to know. And she did.

Hannah and Brid, who were already the best of friends, again became inseparable especially whenever Hannah traveled. She was happy that Brid had not forgotten how to talk while he was away with Kaye. He and Shadow were forever hangout buddies anyway, so the trio was back together. They had done their work.

Ben and Cora had other babies and watched the stars and anyone who visited the house next door and across the street. People often commented about how they never changed and often looked younger each time they saw them. They missed Hannah, but knew she was not theirs to keep, so they just continued.

Professor Belford Stevens moved in next door from time to time, taking over Jacob's house. To the neighbors he was Jacob's eccentric grandfather, staying there while Jacob worked in other cities, working through the pain of losing his wife, Grace.

Everyone still talks about the first night Stevens had moved in and the roof blew off and the walls caved in. It looked as though they were performing on stage with the neighbors as an audience. Pawpaw and Ben got rid of Baxter's spirit and many of the others that night. People still bring up how they heard a commotion, and swear that smoke and fire ran straight out of the roof towards the sky, then, it was gobbled up by a cloud and vanished into nothing. When the fire department and police showed up, Stevens and Ben were sitting at the table playing chess and the roof was intact along with the rest of the house.

Stevens asked innocently, "Can I help you officers?" as they walked through the open entryway.

There was nothing there for them to investigate except two old fogies with a board game and a bottle of scotch between them.

Kaye visited there from time to time. She and Stevens would just plain disappear, or show up in the back yard with an entourage of travel buddies, then leave no evidence they'd ever been there.

Jacob was quite okay with the future and understood his role in keeping things in constant change while not disturbing things in the past. Although many times he wanted to change the awful things that happened in the world, he understood the consequences of attempting that change.

Lily continued playing her cello and working on simple projects to make the world better and in travel spoke of the good people could contribute to mankind. Sometimes her writing was discovered in places that were a bit odd, but never the less well read and circulated.

Jacob and Lily, they were quite a match. They traveled and saw things, and helped things work, and interfered with progress at times, and in other cases contributed to new thought and discovery. They made many babies together and wrote stories and wrote poetry and sang songs and danced. And they did not live happily ever after, but in spite of everything, they tried to.

There is no end.

Also available from PublishAmerica

BEHIND THE SHADOWS
by Susan C. Finelli

Born into squalor, Raymond Nasco's quest for wealth and power shrouds two generations with deceit, murder, rape and illicit love. Setting his sights above and beyond the family's two-room apartment in a New York City lower eastside tenement, Raymond befriends Guy Straga, the son of a wealthy business tycoon, and they develop a lifelong friendship and bond. Caught in Raymond's powerful grip, his wife, Adele, commits the ultimate sin; and his son, Spencer, betrays himself and the woman he loves and finally becomes his father's son. Years later Kay Straga stumbles upon the secret that has been lurking in the shadows of the Straga and Nasco families for two generations, a secret that tempts her with forbidden love, a secret that once uncovered will keep her in its clutches from which there is no escape.

Paperback, 292 pages
6" x 9"
ISBN 1-4241-8974-8

About the author:

Susan C. Finelli has lived in New York all of her life and has been a Manhattanite for over thirty years. She, her husband John, and Riley Rian, their beloved cavalier King Charles spaniel, currently reside in Manhattan, and together they enjoy exploring the sights, sounds and vibrancy of the Big Apple.

Available to all bookstores nationwide.
www.publishamerica.com